SOUL KEEPER

JAMELL PONDER

TATE PUBLISHING
AND **ENTERPRISES**, LLC

Published by Tate Publishing & Enterprises, LLC
127 E. Trade Center Terrace | Mustang, Oklahoma 73064 USA
1.888.361.9473 | www.tatepublishing.com

Tate Publishing is committed to excellence in the publishing industry. The company reflects the philosophy established by the founders, based on Psalm 68:11,
"The Lord gave the word and great was the company of those who published it."

Book design copyright © 2016 by Tate Publishing, LLC. All rights reserved.
Cover design by Norlan Balazo
Interior design by Caypeeline Casas

Published in the United States of America

ISBN: 978-1-68301-979-4
1. Fiction / Christian / Fantasy
2. Fiction / Action & Adventure
16.05.30

SOUL
KEEPER

To Aleah, the god-child and my niece,
Journey that I have been blessed with the opportunity
to love. May You always walk in the path God has
designed, and may the adults in your lives always be
the example you need. Love you just because...

Prologue

—∞—

The darkness pierced through the night, and as foretold, evil lurked about. Shay was not a believer in the notion of urban legends, but something didn't feel quite right.

The rain dropped onto the windowsill, and Shay could feel the coming of pain as he rolled out of bed and padded to the kitchen. Unable to sleep, he rolled the curtains back and stared through the windowpane.

The black clock on the kitchen wall read 2:30 a.m. The red second hand appeared to move in slow motion as Shay thought about all his responsibilities for the day that was slowly approaching.

He was excited to take Aleah to the circus. She had been talking about going for such a long time now that he absolutely had to take her. There was no backing out. Aleah sure knew how to make Shay feel guilty for not keeping his word. "Oh, I thought it was bad to tell lies?" she'd ask in a cynical tone.

"I really have to get some sleep," Shay said as he attempted to turn his thoughts off.

Shay continued to watch the tireless defy the night and the sleepless forsake their rest. The cars periodically drove by; the rude honked horns while screaming obscenities out of their inebriated and foul mouths.

These imbeciles are reckless. Tragic, to be honest, Shay thought to himself. *They're gonna kill somebody sooner or later.*

The wind smashed violently against the house, and the water continued painting the house clear. Shay looked out the window once more. His core crumbled as he thought, *Something just isn't quite right tonight.*

Shay closed his eyes and felt the gunshots leave the unknown gun.

The screams were ferocious, and the fear was soul gripping. The pain ripped Shay away and into another place. A single tear fell from his eyes. He laid his head on his kitchen table, where his mobile phone lay. The ringing of the phone startled Shay back to reality. "Ummmmm…" The preceding silence was far more lethal than whatever words would follow.

1

---~m~---

"I've been waiting for you."

"You know if you ever need me, I'll be there for you. But..."

"But what, Shay?"

Shay continued after the long and involuntary pause. "What have you been waiting for?"

"I've been waiting to see you one last time, talk to you one last time before..."

The tears streamed down the cheeks of the man who loved stronger than any other. "What do you mean one last time?" he asked.

"One last time before I go to be with our Father."

Shay sat in silence and in awe of the certainty with which Aleah spoke.

"I see really bright lights, Shay. It looks so, so, so awesome!" five-year-old Aleah spoke.

Shay looked toward the heavens; he sniffled at the overwhelming moment before his eyes.

"Don't cry, Shay!"

Shay wiped his tears away. "Aleah, I desperately need you to know that I've always loved you deeper than any other.

From the time God formed you in your mother's stomach, I longed to see you, to know you, to love you, and…"

"Shay, I know. How could I not know?"

Shay laughed. "I need you to also know that you've always been the apple of my eye…my heart. From before you saw your first daylight, you've been in my heart, and there you will always remain. I don't want you to go. I'd give my life for yours this very moment in which I speak…"

"I have to go home so other kids can come here. Shay, you're super amazing, and you've loved me just the way I needed, but now I get to watch you from above, smiling as I watch you love other kids just the way they need you to."

"But I want to love you and hold you and make you the happiest little girl alive!"

"I *am* the happiest little girl alive. And you can always love me in your heart. I will always be there."

"I understand your strength, but…"

Aleah closed her eyes. "Shay?"

"Yes?"

"I love you, Dad." She smiled. "Good-bye for now!" Aleah closed her eyes to rest—a rest that felt like death was sure to come.

2

—∞—

Her eyes closed, signaling her temporary good-bye to the people and world she had come to love. The visitors wept. Shay lay next to the motionless body of the child he loved. "Get out of that bed," little Journey said through her clogged throat.

Others were oblivious, but Shay heard the footsteps of the unwelcome. He lamented in a realm far beyond the known. His heart broke from the hefty weight resting upon it. Usually a profound problem solver, Shay now faced the problem with no foreseeable solution. Indemnification was unattainable!

"Uncle Shay! Uncle Shay…get up! Get up out of that bed. She's gone…" little Journey cried.

Guests shook their heads. Hopeless, helpless, and at a loss for words, they watched as the scene unfolded.

"*No!*" Shay yelled through tears. He rolled out of bed and staggered to the door.

"Where is he going?" everyone asked in their own way among the chaotic chatter.

Shay was met at the door by a light-skinned man in a long coat.

"Why are you here?" Shay asked.

"I've come to move the body of this comatose child!"

Aleah had been placed into a medically induced coma to protect her heart.

"Well, I am searching for the soul." Shay wept.

"I'm sorry…"

"You're…sorry?" Shay asked.

"Yes, but…"

Shay pushed the stranger back. "Let's talk about the magnitude of your failure! Aren't you a doctor?"

The stranger remained quiet.

"Fine…don't talk!"

"Get out of my way. I have a body to deliver," the stranger replied.

"Who are you?"

"That is not your concern."

"Step back!"

"Listen, she's simply another statistic, a victim of fate."

"You know something?"

The man lifted his clipboard and seemed to ignore Shay's question.

Shay clenched his fist, raised it up, and cocked it back.

The man raised his eyebrows, lowered his glasses, and smirked. "I'll give you all more time!"

He disappeared into the distance.

3

Shay paced the hallway for what felt like hours. Just then, through the window, a building that stood long before Shay's entry into the hospital now magnified before Shay's eyes. "Who has an office at the top of a building?"

After navigating the maze of the building, he found himself at the hospital's side door exit.

He treaded through the mud as the raindrops fell on his face. Now that he'd walked the dreadful path through a nonliteral, fictitious Hell, he longed for the God in Heaven.

Wow, that door is huge, and that is surely a tall building! Shay said to himself.

Shay banged and banged, yelled then banged some more, but to no avail. Minutes—maybe an hour or so—passed, and Shay finally got through the door.

"There must be a million steps in this stairwell!"

As Shay looked as far as his natural eyes could, he noticed the disappearing darkness. The light gradually approached, and admittedly, Shay hadn't a clue about what he'd gotten himself into. Nevertheless, he carried on, one step at a time.

He moved closer and could now see the silhouette of a man at the top of the stairwell.

"Oh, great—another barrier!"

Shay paused then continued on his exhausting and ambiguous journey. He thought of all he'd left behind for this perilous fight.

"Uncle Shay!" Once again, he heard the voice of his niece, little Journey.

I can't turn back now! he thought to himself as he shook his head from side to side.

As he drew nearer, he heard the voice of the gatekeeper who guarded the door.

"You can't come in here!" the gatekeeper said.

"I can and I will!" Shay responded.

The gatekeeper turned on the bright light wrapped around his forehead. His white jacket flowed like the wavy hair of a beautiful woman. He began moving his hand toward his hip.

"Listen, I need to see the director of this god-awful place!"

"I'm so sorry, sir, but the director only speaks with people by appointment or personal request!" the gatekeeper said as he looked Shay up and down.

"Okay, I am getting really, really annoyed, and this is urgent, so get out of my way!" Shay responded.

"People who are this upset about outcomes in places like this usually pray. Sir, you should try it!"

"First of all, learn my name. Second of all, move, or I am going to—"

"You're going to what?" the gatekeeper interrupted.

"I am going to push right through you!"

"You're definitely not! Leave now, sir!"

Shay inched closer. "Move! If you will not move, then you leave me no choice but to—"

Shay suddenly shoved the man against the door. The guard propelled himself forward. "Leave! You cannot get into this office without an appointment."

"Get—out—of my—way!" Shay said aggressively as he reached for the coat sleeves of the guard, otherwise known as the gatekeeper.

The guard pulled back then pushed Shay away. "Get out of here!"

Shay stumbled and almost fell down the stairs but managed to regain his balance. "I'm getting in to see the director!"

"No, you're not. Now listen here—"

"I am going to punch through your face if you do not step aside. I am talking to the director whether you or anyone else likes it or not. You incompetent flunkies let my goddaughter die. I want answers, and I want them now!" Shay said as he clenched both fists, interrupting the gatekeeper.

The gatekeeper tilted his head slightly to the right and smirked. "People die here all the time. Leave!"

"Not her, not now, so move!"

Before Shay could utter his next words, he felt a .380 pistol pointing at and touching his forehead.

"Do not, I repeat, do not make me add to this grief," the gatekeeper said aggressively.

"I will die for her in a heartbeat," Shay responded.

"Fine then! Have it your way!"

Shay pushed his forehead forward against the gun. Then, before Shay could blink one more time or think one more thought, it happened.

Bang!

The light faded.

4

—∞—

Our life is but a vapor. We are here today, but tomorrow has never been promised to anyone. The only one capable of preserving or exterminating life is God himself. His grace and mercy is inevitably placed on trial anytime a loved one is lost forever. Rightfully so, we question the God we've come to understand. The box we've put God in determines what we believe he can and should do. Our view of God serves to guide what we consider his power to be.

The Serenity prayer says, "God grant me the serenity to change the things I can, to accept the things I can't, and the wisdom to know the difference," though Shay did not subscribe to this. For him, desire for change was greater than the reality of present circumstances.

Life is but a vapor though the fight for preservation is perilous and futile, but perhaps God hears the prayers of the mournful and invokes his grace when moved enough to do so.

5

—⚬—

A loud and deep voice spoke, "Let this man in."

"Thank you. It's about time," Shay said as he brushed the wrinkles from his shirtsleeve.

"You labored long and hard to get here. Now what?" the director asked.

"Uncle Shay!" little Journey yelled.

Through the white noise in and around him, Shay could hear her cries.

"I can't turn back now!" Shay looked at the door. "I'll be there, little Journey."

"I am waiting, sir," the director said impatiently.

"Well, I thought you had power, compassion, and the ability to save lives."

"I do."

"Then why is my goddaughter facing death?" Shay asked almost rhetorically.

"If she's facing death, then why are you here?" the director asked.

"You're in no position to be cynical. I will sue your sorry—"

"Save it! I am the law!" the director said.

"Okay, Mr. Law, you have two options!" Shay said as he stared the director square in the eyes.

"You're giving *me* options?" The director scrunched the left side of his face, partially closing one eye.

"Um, yeah! Either give my goddaughter her life back, or…"

Shay delivered his partial offer.

"This is the most absurd conversation I have ever had, and I've been in the business for a very long time. People ask a lot of me, but this is…" The director took a deep breath. "Never mind. So what is number two?"

"You don't want to know, Mr. Law!"

"Sir, my question wasn't rhetorical," the director said in a calm voice. "What's the point of telling me that I have two options if you're only going to inform me of one?"

"Maybe you'd like to start by learning my name. Certainly, it isn't *sir*. Are you at least ready to learn my name?" Shay asked.

"So tell me your name!"

"I'll take that as a yes. The name is Shay."

"Nice to meet you, Shay."

"What is your name, Mr. Director?" Shay asked.

"Just call me Doc," the director replied.

"Well…Doc, we all need your help!" Shay said.

"Shay, I am really sorry, but she is simply a victim of fate, and you must accept that. And by *all*, I am assuming that you mean family and friends connected with this little girl, Aleah."

"Forgive me, Doc, but I see miracles all the time. Oh, and yes, I do mean friends and family that are connected to Aleah. I see doctors work wonders all the time. I do not mean to sound agnostic, but where is God now? Where are your best doctors when they are needed most? No, I will not accept this!" Shay pounded both fists on the desk. "How do you know her name anyways, Doc?" Shay continued.

"If I were God, I'd answer all of your questions. And by the way, I know everything!" Doc said.

"Fortunately for you, you're the closest I can get to God right now. So you'd better start answering! Since you know everything, you must know what I am going to do to you," Shay responded.

"With your attitude, why would I want to help you anyway?" Doc asked.

"Because I am this close to becoming your worst nightmare," Shay replied.

"And, Shay, I am this close to throwing you out of my haven," Doc said.

Shay was silent.

"Guards? Gatekeeper?" Doc called out.

"Yes, Doc?" the guards and the gatekeeper responded simultaneously.

"Get this man out of my presence!"

"All right, mister, let's go!" the gatekeeper said as he inched closer to Shay.

"No, not yet!" Shay yelled.

As the guards approached Shay, he stood firm, determined not to move. "I am…not going…any…where until your director…does…something!"

Two guards grabbed hold of Shay's arms. The guards—one black male and one white female—screamed in an unfamiliar tongue and language. The gatekeeper—a black man—Shay resisted but unsuccessfully. The facade of anger had fallen, anxiety and sadness overwhelmed him then fear evoked an alternate response. Shay pleaded for one productive conversation.

"I just need to talk," Shay said in a passive-assertive manner.

The guards held firm and moved closer to the door of the million-step stairwell.

An Asian female guard stepped out from around the sharp corner and opened the steel door.

Shay fought back tears but thought quickly about a way to change the situation.

"Wait!" Doc spoke.

The murmuring among the guards ensued and erupted further.

"Give this man one more opportunity to express himself!"

"Aw, come on, let us throw this vagabond back to where he belongs! Why would you indulge this man?"

"I have spoken!" Doc continued.

Shay shook his arms loose of all the tension created from the tussle. He smiled with gratitude. "Thanks, Doc. Now let me start over."

"Please excuse us, guys. Continue, sir."

"I just do not want to lose her. Since I found out that God had blessed her mother with her, I've wanted nothing more than to protect her." Shay wiped his tears then continued, "I've been her guide, her guard, her teacher, and her smile."

"Be proud of that, Shay."

"But I feel like I failed her," Shay said angrily. "What godfather watches his godchild die and does nothing to stop it?"

"I understand your frustration, but you are not in control of life and death," Doc said candidly.

Shay continued to cry. "Her smile is my sunshine, and when I show up, I make her smile. I just want to see her smile again."

"I am really sorry, sir," the director said in a matter-of-fact tone.

"She is fighting so hard. I just hope she doesn't lose and die so young." Shay fell to his knees, and the tears fell faster. "One moment, we were laughing and playing, and"—Shay tried wiping his tears as best he could—"and…and one moment, we were talking then, in an instant, it all changed. My sweet Aleah was simply a young girl fighting for her life. Her young life was sucked into, absolutely the wrong realm." Shay paused. "Do you have children, Doc?"

"Yes, I do. I have one son, but I feel like a father to many."

"So you understand what I am going through?" Shay asked as he rose back to his feet.

"Indeed, sir. He was actually murdered."

"I am really sorry to hear that, Doc. But listen, she deserves to live. Please do not let her become another statistic like your son. She is such a good kid with such a sweet spirit. Doc, I just want her to pull through."

Doc wiped a tear, lowered his glasses, and looked at Shay. "Death comes to all. We just have to go through our range of emotions, our typical stages of grief. We can memorialize the deceased, but rebirth is improbable unless God himself is feeling especially gracious. The best that I can offer at this point is that we wait."

Shay shook his head. "It's just not fair…just not fair, Doc!"

"This isn't about fairness. My son was murdered. Do you think that was fair?" Doc laid his pen on the desk. "It's about reality. And the reality is that people die, they leave us, and sometimes they never come back."

"Hey, Doc, I understand what you're saying. I am so sorry about your son, but can you just rush deliver her a new heart?"

"I am so sorry, Shay, but the list of patients is long and the list of donors short."

"So there's nothing you can do?"

Doc shook his head. "I am really sorry, but I do not think so."

In silence, Shay sat.

"Why her?" the director asked.

"I was ordained by God to love, lead, and protect her. It was only by divine ordination that I am in her life."

"Well, do you feel you've lived up to your responsibilities?"

"As best I could," Shay replied.

Doc smiled. "I wholly admire your heart and passion for the well-being of this child. But why don't you try to find joy in the fact that you gave her the best you had to offer?"

"Because if she dies this way, then all that I've done wasn't enough. It was in vain!" Shay replied.

"Why do you feel that way, Shay?" Doc asked.

"Because in the end, I couldn't save her. I couldn't save her, Doc!" Shay shook his head in frustration.

"Oh no, no, no, no." Doc waved his index finger. "You're not God. You cannot blame yourself for something only God controls. If she dies, it is no fault of yours, sir."

"I'm only human. I am imperfect. I try but often fail. I put my best foot forward, and more times than not, it isn't enough. I have taken thousands upon thousands of steps forward, but you know what?" Shay asked.

"What?" Doc replied.

Shay delivered his disheartening statement: "It is always the one step back that hurts the most."

"If you did your best, then that's what you have to find comfort in."

"There has to be something else!"

"In the end, the something else always expires. Sometimes, there is nothing else." The director offered rationalization amid hurt and confusion.

"I cannot accept that. Nope, Doc, I won't accept that!" Shay replied shortly.

"Your faith is almost unfathomable, sir."

"That's all I have, Doc. All I have."

"You have memories. You have the ability to love other children," Doc said in a quiet tone. "And sometimes, Shay, faith is all that you need."

"Nothing or no one can replace what she means to me," Shay said definitively.

"And, sir, nothing or no one has to," Doc replied.

"Doc, I love many other children, but I am not strong enough to lose Aleah. I am not ready to never see, never hold, or never play with her again."

"I fear you shall die of a broken heart."

"If she dies, Doc, my death is in order!"

"Shay, your life is worth living. There is so much good you have left to do. I see your heart and your compassion. Your empathetic nature is highly respectable, sir. There must be many people God still desperately needs you to touch."

"With her gone, I feel as good as dead."

"But you are very much alive. Don't let loss cause you to lose," Doc said.

"Lose what, Doc?" Shay asked.

"Do not let your loss cause you to lose sight of who you are and why you're here," Doc told Shay.

Shay looked up toward the ceiling. "Just give her back… please!" He dropped back to his knees, wailing in a manner that men typically avoid. "Who are you, God? Who takes a child away at such a young age? When your son—quote unquote—died, you brought him back to life. Ironically enough, your miracle-working powers seem to have fallen short this time."

"Wow, you are pretty bold, challenging the Almighty God," Doc replied.

"Well, the 'Almighty God' isn't seeming so mighty right now, Doc," Shay replied.

"Faith compels." Doc tilted his head slightly to the left.

"Huh? Faith compels?" Shay ruminated on this statement and rehearsed it several times over.

"The intentions of the Almighty are definitely good. Sometimes, things happen that you may not understand, but he always has a plan."

"Easy for you to say, Doc," Shay responded.

"Attitude is everything."

"Well, Doc, I am leaving soon. I suppose I have given my best shot here."

"I see your heart, and mine breaks at the thought of the pain you are experiencing."

"Thanks, Doc." Shay tipped his hat and began walking toward the door. "Doc, would you happen to have an elevator?"

"Wait! Just a second, sir—"

"Shay. My name is Shay."

"I'm sorry, Shay. I want you to meet someone though," Doc responded.

"Okay," Shay said obligingly.

Not long after the exchange of words, a long-legged woman with medium-length hair and fair skin, walked into the room. Her hair flowed like soft wind. The smile upon her face illuminated the room. "Good evening, hon. Who is this fine young gentleman here in your office?" the woman asked.

"Glad you asked, Mona. This is Shay," Doc replied.

Mona stretched out her hand.

"Shay, this is my wife. I call her Mona the Beautiful."

"Nice to meet you, madam." Shay extended his hand.

"Oh, please, call me Mona," Mona said as she grasped hands with Shay.

"Oh, I meant no disrespect. It is a pleasure to meet you, Mona," Shay responded.

"So what brings you to our humble abode?" Mona asked.

"Ah, just fighting for the life of my godchild."

"Oh, I am so sorry. I did hear of that horrific accident." Mona demonstrated empathy for the pain she knew Shay felt.

Shay closed his eyes as the emotions became increasingly overwhelming.

6

S hay remembered waking from his restful sleep when gunshots disturbed the tranquility governing the previous night.

Shay awoke and got ready for work. He had the television playing, but it was only background noise to accompany the usual busyness of the morning. There was nothing intriguing airing on the screen. In a moment, that changed.

"Amber Alert! Amber Alert!" The morning program was interrupted. Shay looked for a moment but then continued preparing for the day.

Shay heard the following words faintly as he was walking away, "A little girl..." Shay moved further away from the screen and toward the remote.

"She is said to be approximately—"

Shay turned off the television, grabbed his car keys, and hurried to the door.

Shay got in his 2013 Honda Accord sedan and cranked the engine. Shay turned the music a notch louder then looked around at all the law enforcement activity—presumably related to the Amber Alert. The ringing of Shay's cell phone startled him, reminding him that he was driving and needed to pay attention to the road.

The window of time for Shay to answer his cell phone had expired. Shay coasted along. He moved his hand toward his cell phone after turning down the music. He didn't see the pickup truck speed through the red light. There was a loud crash as the pickup truck hit a nearby building. The pickup truck flipped several times, and Shay's car turned 360 degrees as he attempted to avoid the collision that was quickly approaching. It was a great attempt but to no avail. Shay's car was turned bottom side up after T-boning the pickup truck. The little girl inside the pickup truck bounced from side to side like a volleyball being tossed about.

"Hello, you've reached my voice mail. Leave your name and number, and I will make certain to return your call at my earliest convenience."

A woman began speaking after the tone. "Shay! Shay! Pick up, it's…"

The sirens sounded as emergency response teams rushed to the scene of the accident. The driver of the pickup truck filled his lungs with air and let out a gasp of breath. He tried pulling himself out of the truck so that he could flee before police arrived.

The onlookers yelled in mass hysteria and disbelief at the scene before their eyes.

"Is that Amber?" one little kid yelled.

Shay passed in and out of consciousness. During one of his moments of consciousness, he heard one of the onlookers say, "I think that's the little girl from the news on channel 12 this morning."

Do I die a legend? Or live akin to a hero? Shay asked himself through soul-crippling fear.

The presumed kidnapper tried planning his escape, but the accident had done more damage than originally calculated. As he attempted to inch out of the damaged and shattered window, the paramedics pulled him out, put him on the stretcher, and assured him that he would be all right.

"Hey, get your hands off of me. I am fine, and I need to leave now," the kidnapper said frantically.

"I am sorry, but I cannot let you leave. We are required by law to conduct a complete medical exam to assure your safety and health," the paramedic responded.

"Move!" the long-haired Caucasian man said as he pushed the emergency response team aside.

"9-1-1, what is your emergency?"

"The driver of the dark-blue pickup truck is slowly fleeing the horrific accident that recently occurred on the corner of Fifth and Reynolds Boulevard. The child is likely to die, but we have reason to believe that this is the little girl for which the Amber Alert was sent this morning," one member of the emergency response team told the 911 operator.

"Okay! Please keep an eye on him. Officers have been dispatched."

The man inched along slowly, but before getting very far, the officers arrived.

"Put your hands in the air, sir!" one officer yelled.

With his back facing the officers, the man stopped right where he stood.

"I said put your darn hands in the air," the officer demanded.

The man raised one hand while the other slowly moved toward his hip.

"Your…other…hand!" The officers stood with guns drawn.

The man quickly turned around while saying, "Show me your hands, idiots!" His face bore an imbalanced expression of desperation, hate, fear, and indifference. He began pulling the trigger and left the officers no choice but to defend themselves. It was his life or theirs.

They shot to kill. One bullet hit his chest. He stumbled back. Another struck the arm with which he held the gun. The arm jerked, and the gun flew far from his reach. The man fell on his back and rolled once.

Life is usually unpredictable, and tomorrow is not promised. The pain was strong, the heart was weak, yet adrenaline constantly remained his driving force, his motivation for destruction. He reached for the gun, and the officers yelled, "Do not grab that gun, sir!"

"Screw you, you stupid pigs!" The man muttered the obscene words he subconsciously knew were his last.

His hand now touched the gun. Self-homicide, suicide by cops, and murder was the story his face foretold. Hatred ushered him without prejudice to his demise.

One shot after the other rang out as the officers delivered what was presumably the fatal shot as his head jolted high then smashed to the ground.

"Paramedics!" one officer yelled.

The emergency response team was scattered about, but all rushed to their respective places.

7

"Is the little girl breathing yet?" one member from the emergency response team asked.

The paramedics communicated with one another as they moved about, quickly using all possible methods to save a life.

Shay suffered injuries, mostly minor, but some were worth further examination at the hospital. Paramedics ran preliminary tests while getting ready for transport.

Something felt distastefully painful about the child struggling for her next breath. Shay looked, but quickly turned away.

"Give me the oxygen!" one of the paramedics yelled.

They pressed and pumped, jolted, and applied other strategic first aid and cardiopulmonary resuscitation techniques learned at a time books were their masters.

"Give me the AED!" one of the paramedics yelled.

A feeling of despair hovered over Shay like the black cloud before night fell. His curiosity got the better of him. He turned to look at the scene once more.

"No, it can't be!" Shay said as a single tear fell from his eye.

"Be calm, sir," one of the paramedics responded.

"Let me go. I have to go over there," Shay said.

"I cannot let you do that."

Shay tussled with all his might until he finally broke loose. Shay ran as fast as an injured man could.

The paramedics worked relentlessly. They were attempting to apply the last wire as Shay pushed through the barrier and fell on the child he loved. "Aleahhhhhh!"

Their bodies touched, and energy loose in the universe refocused to join the magic of the moment.

8

Beep! Beep! Beeeeeeeep!

"This is certainly a miracle if I've ever seen one," one of the paramedics yelled.

The onlookers stood amazed at the power of love. Some smiled, some cried, while some just shared the oohs and aahs in harmony with the increasing number of people around them.

The cops had no choice but to extricate Shay so the paramedics could do their job.

Shay lay on the stretcher. He fell into a deep state of sleep. Shay tossed and turned as he sank further into restlessness. The night persisted, and Aleah monopolized Shay's thoughts.

"I wonder what this young man is thinking about," Mona said to her husband, Doc.

"Let the man rest," Doc replied. "I'm sure we will know at some point what troubled his mind as well as what brought him genuine happiness."

"Yes, you are right, honey," Mona responded to her husband's words of wisdom.

"I'd like for you to pay the child a visit and bring me a report on her condition."

"Okay, sweetie," Mona said as she wrapped up tight for her journey across the campus.

9

Mona looked in on the little girl slowly sinking deeper into the realm outside of the world as she's known it. Her soul traveled much farther than expected, for she was but a young child. Her life was short and now fading because of the evil ways of another.

Mona called her husband while still looking in on Aleah, who was clearly remembering something and doing so at the worst of times. "Sweetie, it's not looking so good for this little girl, Aleah. I do not know if we will be able to save her."

The director shook his head with sadness. "Thanks, hon."

"You're welcome," Mona said as she hung up the phone.

Aleah had noticed a strange rusty blue pick-up truck circling the school playground several days before being abducted. But as most children, she was oblivious to any consequential danger that may have been developing.

"Hey, Buck, which little girl looks good to you?" the driver asked as he watched Aleah playing so gracefully and without a worry in the world.

"That little girl right there," Buck replied.

"Which one, idiot? There are a lot of little girls out there," said Harry, the driver.

"The little girl that is about to ride by the long metal slide."

Harry, Buck's friend, looked on with an increasing appetite as Aleah swung about. He had sweet plans for her. He planned to do things to her that she would never forget. If she was still alive after their preordained encounter, Aleah would never forget Harry—or Buck. Harry had already determined that not so deep in his subconscious.

She laughed and played and laughed and played and repeated the process. For Aleah, her world moved in slow motion. She had no inkling about the danger awaiting her.

"Ah, well, Buck, today is Tuesday. What about we return Thursday at the same time?"

"I like that idea."

Aleah's smile and beauty caused the animalistic instincts to erupt inside of Harry. "I will see you soon, little beauty," he said as he smirked.

"Hey, man, we gotta get out of here before someone sees us," Buck said as he tried to distract Harry from the trance he was now under.

The whistle blew loudly, signaling the conclusion of recess. Aleah turned to look. She'd never forget the terrifying moment and the way she felt when her eyes met Harry's.

She went home, and that night, she told her mother of the day's events.

"Hey, Aleah, how was school today?" Elizabeth asked.

"It was so much fun, Mom," Aleah replied.

"Well, tell me more. What did you do?"

"In music, we listened to some guy named Mozart or something like that."

"What about math or English?"

"Ugh, yes, we learned some math and did a little writing, but…"

Elizabeth saw the terror in Aleah's eyes. "But what, honey? You can tell Mommy anything," she said as she put her hand softly on Aleah's back.

"Mommy, there was this mean-looking man in a blue truck watching all of the kids play during recess today."

"Did he hurt you?" Elizabeth asked.

"No, Mommy, but he looked very mean and very scary."

"Well, I'm sure he didn't mean anything by it," Elizabeth said dismissively.

"All right, Mommy. If you are not worried, then I will not worry."

Aleah ran about, playing the evening away until bedtime arrived.

Another day went by, and Aleah felt safer with each passing minute.

Elizabeth had kind of forgotten what Aleah told her two days ago. Her morning was just like any other. She got dressed and ready for her day. She made Aleah breakfast and made sure she was ready when the bus came.

Aleah continued stuffing apple-and-cinnamon oatmeal into her mouth. When she saw the bus drive by and briefly stop, she put another bite into her mouth, then, in defiance of one of her mother's rules, spoke with a mouth full of food. "There goes the bus, Mommy!"

"Aleah, I have asked you many times not to talk with your mouth full. I cannot even understand you."

Aleah swallowed the food in her mouth. "I said there goes the bus," she repeated.

"Oh my, hurry up, Aleah. We have to get out of here," Elizabeth said.

Aleah rushed to put on her jacket then grabbed her backpack and ran toward the door with Mommy.

"Aleah, you missed your bus. Just wonderful! Now I am going to be late to work."

Elizabeth got Aleah to school as fast as she could. "All right, Aleah, hurry up and get into the building."

Elizabeth watched for a moment as Aleah ran toward the front door. Pulling away before she was inside of the door wasn't an unusual practice. As she was turning the corner, she saw a blue pickup truck pulling up to the school.

Her thoughts raced, but she quickly resolved the motion of her mind. "No, I'm just being paranoid. It couldn't be." Elizabeth was in a hurry, so she sent Aleah off and began driving to work.

Bang! A gunshot rang out. The screams were fierce and panic evoked a response—the people scattered.

Elizabeth stopped her car and tried to see what was happening amid the chaos in front of the school.

"Okay, just breathe, Elizabeth," she told herself. "I am just going to call the school and make sure that Aleah reported to class. I am sure she did. My little girl is fine, and as every mother would be, I'm just really worried."

Elizabeth took a deep breath. She then held her breath and counted backward from ten to one while continuing to hold her breath. The time had come. She picked up her cell phone and began calling the school as she paced at a nearby sidewalk.

"Hello, you've reached Every Child Matters Learning Institute. How may I help you?"

"Yes, hello. This is Aleah Prim's mother, Elizabeth. I just wanted to make sure that Aleah reported for class."

"Hold up, Ms. Prim, I will check for you."

Not too long after, she received the worst news of her entire life. Across her cell phone, the message read,

> AMBER ALERT! A GIRL—APPROXIMATELY 5 YEARS OLD WITH BROWN HAIR—HAS JUST BEEN TAKEN BY A WHITE MALE APPROXIMATELY 6 FEET TALL, DRIVING A BLUE PICKUP TRUCK!

"Ms. Prim, are you there?" The silence confused the receptionist. "Um, Elizabeth, are you there?"

Elizabeth dropped her phone in disbelief after the notification about the Amber Alert. "Yes, I am here," Elizabeth said as she quickly picked her phone up from the ground.

"I am sorry, Ms. Prim, but Aleah never—"

Elizabeth couldn't stand to hear the rest. She finished their sentence in her mind and shoved her phone in her purse.

The blue pickup truck appeared to be long gone. Elizabeth stood outside of the truck and outside of herself. "Please, God, tell me my little girl wasn't trying to tell me what I think she was."

She ran back to her car and pulled her cell phone out of her purse. She dialed Shay's number but sadly received no answer. She stepped out of her vehicle again and paced quickly outside of her car. She put both hands on her forehead. "No! This cannot be happening!" Elizabeth said. She got back into her car and turned on the radio news channel 109.5 the Buzz to hear if there had been any new developments.

"Car accident on the corner of Fifth and Reynolds Boulevard. Breaking news, a 2013 Honda, color silver, just T-boned a 1996 blue pickup truck," the reporter said.

"Oh no! Wait a minute? Doesn't Shay drive a silver 2013 Honda Accord?" Elizabeth said to herself. "Not my little girl." Elizabeth wept. "And possibly Shay as well?" She never told Shay, but in the secret of her soul, she longed to be more than just his friend.

She shook her head as she stood immobilized. "Aleah! Shay!" she called out as she fell to her knees on the sidewalk beside her vehicle.

The crowd of people stared. None with the courage to intervene.

"I got to go!" Elizabeth took the back roads and all the shortcuts she knew to arrive as quickly as possible to the scene of the accident. She now stood entranced at the terrifying sight before her eyes.

"Where is my baby?" Elizabeth asked one of the emergency medical personnel.

"Ma'am, I cannot—" one of the paramedics said.

"Shay!" Elizabeth said as she looked at the stretcher.

"Elizabeth, I am so sorry," Shay said.

"What are you talking about?" Elizabeth inquired.

"I am sorry! I tried!" Shay said as he wept, holding his hip with his right hand, his left hand covering his face.

"Please tell me what is going on, Shay!"

Shay looked toward the heavens. "It's Aleah. She was involved in an accident."

"Oh no!" Elizabeth began to weep.

The two embraced, and tears fell.

"Just please tell me exactly what happened!" Elizabeth looked Shay straight in his eyes.

"Okay, I was driving, and the blue pickup truck ran through the red light. We collided, then…"

"Shay…then what?"

Shay took a deep breath. "Then—"

Ring! Ring! Ring! "One second, Shay," Elizabeth said as she wiped tears from her eyes. "Hello, this is Elizabeth Prim."

"Ms. Prim, this is Jacqueline from Brown Memorial Hospital. We have your daughter Aleah, but—"

"Is she okay?"

"I can tell you that she is stable, but—"

"But what?"

"But, ma'am, you must hurry."

Elizabeth quickly hung up the phone. "Let's go, Shay!"

"Elizabeth—"

"I do not have time to waste. You're either coming or not!"

"Let's go," Shay muttered through his aches and pain.

10

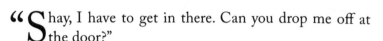

"Shay, I have to get in there. Can you drop me off at the door?"

"Sure."

Elizabeth squealed away and pulled into the nearest spot she could find. She hurried into the hospital and located Aleah's room. "Not my baby!" she cried and yelled from the agony that tortured her.

"Ma'am, I know it's hard, but please try to remain calm."

"Calm? Did you say calm?"

"Are you this young child's mother?"

"Yes, I am!"

"Okay, I need you to take a few deep breaths and relax, if at all possible, so that we can do our job as best as possible."

"My little baby girl is fighting for her life and you tell me to remain calm?"

The silence had little effect on quieting Elizabeth, the irate mother.

"There are tubes and…I don't even know what all of these metal objects are! Don't tell me to remain calm. You save my little girl's life, and then I will remain calm, take a few breaths, and relax, as you put it!"

"Ms. Prim, please wait outside for just a moment."

"What do you mean wait outside?" Elizabeth asked.

"Ma'am, I am just trying to make sure that we can give your little girl the best care possible. It will be easier if all family and friends were outside of the room while we are operating. Do not worry, Ms. Prim, you will be the first person that we notify."

"Okay," Elizabeth said before walking away.

Elizabeth Prim waited for what felt like forever.

Finally, the doctor came to deliver his prognosis. "Ms. Prim, I am sorry, but we have done all that we could do. She is breathing on her own, but I cannot say how much longer she will live. Please call all family who isn't already on the way. I am so very sorry, but treasure these precious moments. They will most likely be her last." The doctor held his head down as he walked away. "There is one recommendation that would preserve her heart temporarily!"

"What is your recommendation?" Elizabeth asked.

"A medically induced coma!"

"Do whatever you have to do in order to save my little girl," Elizabeth spoke through her tears.

Shortly after the doctor's departure, family and friends filed in to see Aleah and, unbeknownst to many of them, say their final good-byes. The hugs and blank stares were plentiful. The "I'm sorrys" and disapproving headshakes were copious just the same.

"Journey, would you like to come with me to see Aleah?" Elizabeth asked.

"Yeah!" little Journey said in a low and dejected voice.

The two of them, among a few others, walked the frightful path to the room in which Aleah lay.

"Hey, Aleah!" Journey awaited a response.

"Are we going to play in the sandbox tomorrow?" After the brief silence.

Journey looked at Elizabeth then at Aleah and back at Elizabeth. Elizabeth nodded for her to say whatever she felt in her little heart.

Journey began to weep. "Aleah is sleeping, Journey."

Elizabeth turned away to conceal the tears that she couldn't resist.

"It's okay if you cry!" Shay said as he placed his hand on Elizabeth's back.

"Thank you, Shay, thank you so much." Elizabeth said as she looked out the window.

There was a sort of awkward quiet that absorbed the aura of the room.

Aleah heard all that was going on around her. Her fragile heart broke for all of the sadness that surrounded her. She wished that she could hug back, talk back, and love back, but instead, she just lay awaiting a miracle from above.

Journey ran to Aleah's bedside. "I love you, god-cousin."

And I love you, Aleah responded, though only in thought.

Journey frowned, Shay's face was wrought with anger, and Elizabeth's faced puffed from the tears she continued to cry.

"We're not going to play in the sandbox tomorrow!" Journey told herself.

The doctors thought I was sleeping and said I've lost too much blood. They said there was too much damage…well…it was something like that. I'm a little girl. I don't understand big people all the time, but sometimes I do. I'm never going to see my friends and mommy and Shay anymore, Aleah thought. Her leg twitched slightly.

No one knew the right words at such a time as this.

I tried to tell you, Mommy, Aleah thought.

"Aleah tried to warn me!" Elizabeth complained.

It's okay, Mommy. It's not your fault that man was bad, Aleah thought.

"This is not your fault." Shay grabbed Elizabeth's hand.

Elizabeth smiled a little.

All eyes looked at the long-haired man being rolled past Aleah's room. Shay began walking away.

Not long after the murky interruption, the silhouette of a man approached the doorway.

Shay returned several moments later. Sadness without invitation gripped the core of his being. He trembled inside. Beneath the visible showings of anguish, he wished he would awake and shake his head at this horrific nightmare. Did he want to return to what awaited him on the other side of the door? His soul was in turmoil. His mind calculated then recalculated, but the barriers to solutions were too great. His thoughts brought no resolve, but he wondered if the warrior in his soul would arise.

Aleah smiled inside, and then thought, *I've been waiting for you.*

11

—⟊—

Shay hobbled back into the room, grimacing from his minor injuries. Aleah sensed Shay's return. He was inadvertently shoved to the floor, and she heard, "Where is my baby? Get out of my way!"

"Hey, you haven't even been around! Do not come in here pushing past people! Especially people that have been consistent in her life!" Elizabeth stopped Henry, Aleah's biological father, right where he stood.

Meanwhile, Shay pulled himself to his feet.

"Well, I am here now, Elizabeth. I came as soon as I got news of the accident."

"What about every other day of her life?"

Hey, guys, I can hear you, Aleah thought.

"Let's talk about this outside," Elizabeth said.

They stepped outside the door to finish what had begun in the room.

"Listen, I am sorry, all right?" Henry said.

"All right," Elizabeth responded.

"But this is not the time to discuss this," Henry continued.

"Fine, but do not think it was ever all right that you always walked in and out of her life."

"We'll talk later," Henry said as he pushed past Elizabeth. He stood at the door, watching as his Shay spoke words that he envied.

I've been waiting for you, Aleah thought.

"You know if you ever need me, I'll be there for you. But…"

"Hey, baby," Henry interrupted.

Hi, Daddy, Aleah thought to herself. No one knew how desperately she wished she could talk to them.

Henry began to tear up a bit. "Everything is going to be just fine," he said as he rubbed Aleah's hand.

Daddy, no. Everything will not be just fine, Aleah thought. *Dad, sometimes you just know what's going to happen,* Aleah's thoughts continued.

"I am going to step outside for a moment." Henry walked out as the emotions of the moment were too difficult, and he did not want to cry in front of Aleah.

Henry silently dropped his tears. He did the only thing he knew to do—pray. He sat in the waiting room, bowed his head, and began to speak. "God, if you are real, I need a sign. Save my little baby girl. She doesn't deserve to die this way. I know you've worked many miracles. Don't forsake my little girl in her time of need. I believe in your sovereignty, but undeniably, in this moment, my faith increases or decreases according to your action." Henry paused. "Or your inaction."

A little girl put her hand on Henry's shoulder as she was walking by. Henry stopped and looked. "I think that's…"

"I'm going to go say hi to Aleah again," little Journey said as she walked by with her mother.

Henry smiled as much as he could with the ever-present pain that ran deep. He prayed a little while longer. He felt the weight of hopelessness lift, though only slightly. He looked in on Aleah and noticed Shay lying next to her.

Weird. But whatever heals my little girl's heart. Henry took the nearest seat. "Do you think she'll be all right?" he asked Elizabeth.

They embraced.

"All we can do now is pray," Elizabeth said.

"Get up, Uncle Shay," little Journey warned.

12

―〜〜―

S hay opened his eyes in an inverse reality. "Where am I?"
"You never left our office," Mona replied.

"I really fell asleep?" Shay asked.

"Yes, you did," Doc replied.

Shay shook his head in disbelief.

"Well, with a heart as broken as yours, we thought it best to let you rest," Mona said.

"Call me tomorrow, Shay, and I will give you my final update," Doc said.

"Okay, Doc." Shay put on his jacket, hat, and gloves and began the tedious journey back to the hospital.

His heart hurt more than anyone could possibly know. He'd tried as best as he could to find a solution for Aleah. Bitterness disintegrated the calm and compassionate demeanor that usually defined him. The journey was dreadful as he did not know exactly what would greet him at his final step. Facing the silence was harder than the noise of the night. Was he ready for her last breath?

Shay looked inside of himself to embrace the genuineness of fate. He walked down the stairs to the doorway and began his journey home. He stopped into the hospital to see Aleah lying in a room with a few others. He desperately wanted to hear her voice, but that simply wasn't an option.

The drive home was truly the longest ride.

Shay sat in darkness and lamented over the tragedy that plummeted the dagger through his heart. He turned on his bedroom light and flipped through pictures, though the reminiscing simply produced more pain. Five years was a short time, though the memories made five years feel like fifty years. His love for her would never end. Replacement was never considered because some people are truly irreplaceable. Their bond was forever irrevocable. Shay was a guy who brought to pass the promises he made, but there was only one God controlling life and death. He'd find a plan. He'd find a way.

"I am your worst enemy, God. You failed so many people. I thought you were all powerful. I'll confront the real power. Just you wait."

Shay was usually someone who operated as a realist, but he was determined to defy natural law. He set his mind to overcome this law of natural consequences. He could see no limits to the power of love. He refused to give up the fight. He tried to rest, but his mind would not allow it. He took ZzzQuil, but his thoughts outraced the intended impact of the substance. Dreams became nightmares, nightmares became the norm, and fear became the reality. The reality was that he was losing Aleah, and he did not want to accept the truth, to face the pain; neither did he want to wake to experience life without her. Things were about to drastically change but not without the fight of his life. The ultimate dream would precede the desperate measures he'd purposed in his mind to take.

13

—〰—

Nightmares were the very reason Shay hated falling asleep. He remembered it all this way:

"Hey, Shay," Elizabeth said excitedly.

"Hello there, Liz," Shay said in a manner that emphasized his curiosity. "Why are you so excited?"

"I'm pregnant!"

They had been friends for three years, so he'd developed a certain amount of protectiveness over her. "Okay, so who is the father?"

Shay thought that Elizabeth was beautiful. He was somewhat jealous that Elizabeth was carrying another man's child. Though whatever feelings he felt, he would not act on them because he feared ruining their friendship that innocently began in college.

"I will give you one guess," Elizabeth responded.

"I'm afraid that I will guess right. Just tell me."

"Nope, you've got to guess!" Elizabeth said.

"Come on, Liz, just tell me, please," Shay pleaded.

"Fine then, it's Henry."

Elizabeth had confirmed Shay's fear and made it a reality.

"Really? Henry? I thought you were done with that guy," Shay said.

"I was, but he talked his way right back into my life," Elizabeth explained.

"And apparently into your pants, Liz," Shay continued.

"Stop it, Shay," Elizabeth said.

"What?" Shay said in an upset tone. "I am just speaking the truth, Liz. And because I love you, I want what's best for you."

"I know, and I always appreciate your advice."

"I'm trying to tell you that he is no good for you."

"I think things will be different this time," Elizabeth said.

"I will get my tissues and my shoulder ready for when you come crying," Shay said, introducing cynicism and sarcasm into the conversation.

Elizabeth was silent as she pondered Shay's words.

"Have you even told him yet?" Shay asked.

"No, you were the first person I called. I am going to see my mom later today. Will you come with me to tell her?"

"Of course, that's what friends are for," Shay said as he smiled.

"Uh, what are friends for?" Elizabeth asked an almost rhetorical question.

"To be there in the tough times. I love you like a little sister, Liz. I just want the best for you."

"I know, but you totally crushed my spirits about being pregnant. Why couldn't you be the father? Ha! Ha!"

"Um, let me give you one reason."

"I'm listening."

"Because we are friends and not lovers."

"Darn!" Elizabeth smirked, teasing Shay.

"Stop it, Liz. We have bigger problems to worry about than you pretending to flirt with me," Shay demanded.

"All right. Well, meet me at my parent's house in a couple of hours," Elizabeth said.

"Okay, well, I will see you then," Shay replied.

Shay made sure to keep the relationship platonic. They had been there for each other through so much over the nine years (three years prior to her pregnancy and in the five years following) that they'd known each other. They were there for comfort following breakups, advice prior to starting certain romantic relationships, and guidance throughout the duration of these romantic relationships. Their friends and families always thought that they would advance to something far beyond friends, but Elizabeth and Shay genuinely valued their friendship and did not want to ruin it. Shay being in Elizabeth's corner as she delivered the news to her parents was just one example of how supportive they were of each other. They loved each other more than friends, but neither acted on their feelings because of the fear of ruining their friendship.

So Shay sat beside Elizabeth as she told her mother and father that she was expecting. Her father just about fell out of his chair. "Liz, honey, that guy is not good for you. I'm sure it's Henry."

"Yes, Dad, it is," Elizabeth felt ashamed because she hadn't listened to the voice of anyone close to her. She looked at her mother as she contemplated her response.

"Elizabeth, we are disappointed in you, but this is not the time for criticism and the familiar 'I told you so.' Your father and I will be there when you need us." Mom smiled. "And, Shay?"

"Yes, ma'am?"

"Thank you very much for being a great friend to our daughter."

"You're welcome. It has been my pleasure."

They wrapped up the conversation. Mom gave her advice regarding pregnancy but didn't take the plunge into the conversation about her joy of being a grandparent in nine months or so.

Shay and Elizabeth walked toward their cars.

"Hey, Liz, do you want to grab a bite to eat and catch up for a little while?"

"Sure, that sounds nice."

They went to the café around the corner from her parents' house. Over the years, it had become their favorite spot.

For all inquiring minds, these two friends, Shay and Elizabeth, met when she worked at the bookstore and Shay came into the store to market and advertise a book he'd recently finished writing. Elizabeth told him of how she had always desired to write a book. The chemistry between them was beyond natural. Maybe there was minimal interest, but overall, they had the kind of friendship that others yearned for. Everything about them came easily. Before long, they were best friends, and the value of their friendship reached an all-time high. They loved each other in the purest form.

14

—⟶⟶—

"So have you thought of any names yet?" Shay asked.

"No, but maybe you and a few other friends can help me with that."

"Ha! You want my help picking out a name?" Shay said as he laughed a little.

"Yes, I do." Elizabeth said jokingly.

"When will you find out what you're having, a boy or a girl?" Shay asked.

"In a few weeks. But we can choose names for both genders," Elizabeth responded.

"Okay, that's a good idea. So when will you tell Henry?" Shay was full of questions for his pregnant friend.

"I guess I can call him right now," Elizabeth said with much timidity.

"Yeah, the sooner the better. Do not worry, I am here if you need anything," Shay reminded her.

"I have a question for you before I call, though," Elizabeth said, prolonging the dreadful call.

"Ask away," Shay said.

"Will you be the godfather?"

"Of course I will," Shay said with a smile that demonstrated his obvious joy and approval.

"Yay!" Elizabeth said in her usual bubbly voice. "Okay, so here goes."

"Here goes?" Shay asked for clarification.

"I am going to call the infamous Henry now." Elizabeth scrolled through her contacts list and initiated the call.

"Hey, babe," Henry answered, using a smooth tone.

Elizabeth was smitten, and she smiled. "Hey, handsome."

Shay wasn't jealous, but he knew she was headed down a road that led to disappointment and, inevitably, despair. He called it men's intuition, but Elizabeth never quite believed that a man could embody that gift the same way women could.

"So what's up?" Henry asked.

"I have something very important to tell you." Elizabeth paused.

"Well, don't keep me in suspense, sexy," Henry responded.

"Uh, I'm…pregnant."

"Do not try to tell me that I am the father." Henry's tone changed. His tone was less smooth and harsher.

"Wait, are you serious right now?" Elizabeth said, surprised.

"You're just trying to pin this kid on me. I do not know if you've cheated on me or not." Henry delivered another surprising statement.

"Oh my gosh, what is wrong with you? I haven't!" Elizabeth said with noticeable hurt in her voice.

This frustrated Shay because he cared about Elizabeth and always wanted nothing less than for her to be happy and treated with the respect that she deserved.

"I do not believe you," Henry responded.

Silence demonstrated the depth of the pain Henry caused Elizabeth to feel. Shay had heard and seen enough.

"Liz, do you want me to talk?" Shay asked.

"That's what I'm talking about. There's another man there right now!" Henry said.

"Wow! It's Shay, hold up!"

"No, I don't want—"

Henry's voice faded off as Elizabeth removed the phone from her ear as he attempted to tell her that he did not want to talk to Shay.

"Can you stop yelling, Henry?"

"Man, I do not want to talk to you," Henry said to Shay.

"Well, I'd like to talk to you," Shay responded.

"What do you want to talk to me for?" Henry asked.

"Because you're hurting my friend!"

"Are you sure that you and her are only friends?"

"That's a logical but rather stupid question."

"Well, it wouldn't surprise me if you were the one screwing her!"

"Okay, can we change the subject, seriously?"

"I'd like to talk about you screwing my girlfriend," Henry replied.

"For the last time, I'm not having sex with your girlfriend. Maybe you should work on your insecurity issues," Shay replied. "Now, can we talk?"

"Whatever, man. Make it quick, hero," Henry replied sarcastically.

"First of all, there is nothing going on between Elizabeth and me. There never has been."

"How do I know that to be true?" Henry asked.

"It's called trust," Shay responded.

"Yeah, whatever!"

"You're turning one of the happiest days of her life into the most miserable day of her life."

"Maybe you're the father," Henry said cynically.

"I'm not. You are," Shay responded candidly.

Shay continued to speak, but Henry had already disconnected the call.

Elizabeth looked lost, confused, disappointed, and really upset.

"Hey, Elizabeth, you know that I will help you in any way I can," Shay said.

"I know, and I thank you even though it's not your responsibility."

"Hey, you know our slogan…" Shay began.

"But that's what friends are for?" the two said simultaneously and laughed afterward.

Elizabeth and Shay finished their tea and sandwiches and parted ways.

Henry became really distant and eventually stopped talking to Elizabeth. She was heartbroken but not wholly alone. Her parents were a great support. Shay also assisted in any way that he was able to. They'd worked on picking out a name, but none had yet surfaced as the best.

Henry found a way to disappear without a trace. He was destined to be a totally irrelevant factor in the life of his child. Henry was from a broken family system. Because of lack of family structure, walking out on a child was all too familiar to him. He never quite desired a family of his own. The idea of having a child never excited him.

Shay continued being the best friend that he could be. Now he had to figure out how to be the best godfather he could. They finally agreed on a name—Aleah.

Time would never arise as man's best friend. Time always took exactly what it wanted, when it wanted. How do you fight an invisible foe? Only behind the dark veil we call life.

15

—∽∽—

A leah was a pretty good baby, as normal as they come. She'd given Shay his first diaper-changing experience. Occasionally, Shay spent the night at Elizabeth's house only to help her with Aleah, her newborn baby girl. And periodically, in the wee hours of the night when she cried, he had the pleasure of comforting her. He built the kind of bonds that fathers desired to build. One significant fact remained true—he wasn't her biological father. That fact never stopped him from being the best godfather he could be.

Elizabeth and Shay loved the small as well as the big moments. Aleah taking her first step created joy akin to her graduating from high school. They clapped and rose from a bended stance to a standing position. Well, that graduation analogy came into question when she fell after her first few steps. But like any upstanding adults, they encouraged Aleah and helped her to her feet when necessary.

At a young age, Aleah was taught that if she fails, she should always try again. And well, eventually, she was walking like an expert. Praise served as a great motivator. While still at a young age, Shay told Aleah that failure would never be the end of her story and that she would do so many wonderful things if she tried hard enough.

Then she started talking. "Dada."

That was the first word she attempted to say.

Shay and Elizabeth would just stare blankly at each other. There was immense joy in communicating with this quickly maturing young child. But how would they explain to Aleah that Shay was not her dada—her father? And when? Well, for now, they chose to embrace the present beauty of the precious moments they had been given.

As with any normally developing child, Aleah's vocabulary expanded. Her conversations became more involved. And then it was time for the big day, her first birthday party.

The balloons blew with the wind, and the kids ran freely and wildly—though Aleah's run appeared more like a brisk walk, given the short stature of her legs. Journey and Ka'Juan, sister and brother, encircled Aleah while their brother President cried from the stroller.

The smiles on the children's faces that day would be forever cemented in the minds of Shay and many others who watched freedom at its finest, joy at its greatest, and fearlessness at its best.

Aleah stole the show. After all, she was the birthday girl. It was as though the adage, "It's my birthday and I'll cry if I want to?" was being displayed. In the truest of ways, Aleah brought that lyric to life on July 22, 2009, her first birthday. Shay undoubtedly had a soft spot for Aleah, so as soon as she cried, he was right by her side to save her in whatever way she needed.

Elizabeth did not like that very much. She'd reprimand him, and by the time the party ended, Shay had finally learned what many were trying to teach him—the meaning of shaping the autonomy of a child. Smiles were many, cries were few, and laughs were plentiful.

"This is living," Shay said to himself.

The next year passed by rather quickly. Sure, there were 365 days, as with every other year except leap years. Though these 365 days felt more like 182 and a half days. Aleah began walking better. Her understanding of language and use of words increased as well. Her relationship with Shay and her mother developed very well. Henry remained uninvolved. Elizabeth and Shay kept the romance absent from their relationship. Their friendship was much closer than it was a year ago.

Aleah was nearing her second birthday, and concerns about her not knowing her father were gradually surfacing.

"Why can't she just call you daddy?" Elizabeth would ask.

Shay's answer would always be the same: "Because when she gets older and asks who her father is, I do not want to lie. And when she asks why we didn't tell her, I will not be able to bear the pain in her eyes, listen to the cries of her heart, and wipe away the tears I helped cause."

Elizabeth dreaded the call she knew she had to make. Henry! He was such a jerk and nothing like Shay. "Why couldn't Shay just be the father of my child?" she would often ask herself. She never quite understood if she had some undiscovered fantasy about Shay or if she simply saw his inherent fatherlike qualities and wished that Aleah could always benefit from them.

Elizabeth slowly picked up the phone and dialed the number of the true antagonist to Aleah's story.

16

---m---

Henry answered the unidentified phone number. "Hello?"

"Henry?" Elizabeth said as the phone stopped ringing.

"Elizabeth?"

"Yeah, it's Elizabeth."

"Well, I am surprised to hear from you," Henry responded.

"I decided that it was time to call," Elizabeth began.

"Why?"

"Henry, Aleah is your kid. No one else's, and I think you should be involved in her life. She'll be two this year and deserves to know her father."

"I do not think she is my kid."

"Well, all you have to do is take a paternity test, then I will prove it to you," Elizabeth said.

"Fine, you pick the place and I will be there," Henry responded.

Elizabeth called around and found the best price for a paternity test. She didn't mind the $400. The most important thing to her was that Aleah knew who her real father was. She would do her part, but Henry being involved was his decision.

She dreaded the day of the paternity test because she didn't even want to be in the same room with Henry, the guy who disregarded her heart and disappeared out of her life, ultimately leaving her as a single parent. She was ashamed that she had conceived his child, but nevertheless, she felt blessed by having Aleah as her child. A very small part of her thought he may actually step up and be a good father in the life of his child.

Well, the day came, and in terms of a good start, Henry was there. Henry and Elizabeth followed the instructions of the geneticist. However, Henry looked nervous. It was obvious he hoped for the worst—or the best, depending on how he conceptualized and defined a negative result. Unfortunately for them, the test would not yield rapid results. They walked out of the facility expecting a phone call in four to six weeks.

The wait was difficult. Meanwhile, Henry refused to see Aleah. He argued the case that it would do more harm than good to begin building a relationship if it turned out that he wasn't the father. Elizabeth would tell him, "My mom raised me well. She did not raise me up to be promiscuous, so I already know that you're the father."

Henry wasn't a believer. He wanted the proof in the pudding, so to speak.

At five and a half weeks, the one call they'd been waiting for finally came.

17

—⚹—

"Hello?" Henry answered.

"Hello, this is Profound Paternity calling. Is Henry available?"

"This is him," Henry responded.

"We have your results. We will disclose over the phone as well as mail a paper copy of the results for your records."

"Okay, I am ready to get this done and over with."

"Well, Mr. Henry—"

The dead air produced nothing less than fear and worry. Henry awaited the results to the question he hated having to ask. They began revealing the results while Elizabeth sat anticipating her phone call from Profound Paternity.

On another telephone line, Elizabeth finally received her call as well. "Hello, may I ask who is calling?"

"Hi, yes, this is Profound Paternity calling with the results for Aleah Prim. Is Elizabeth Prim available?"

"This is she."

"We have your results. We will disclose over the phone as well as mail a paper copy of the results for your records."

"Okay."

Elizabeth waited patiently. The silence was piercing, and then the staff on the other end of the line began revealing the results.

"In the case of Aleah Prim, Henry Black…"

Elizabeth smiled and prepared herself for the next phone call.

Henry sat alone in his one bedroom apartment. He knew that Elizabeth would be calling at some point. His wait wasn't long at all. His phone rang, and he dreaded every ring, so he eventually answered.

"What?" That was the way Henry answered the phone.

"Henry, why are you being rude?" Elizabeth asked.

"Because I really did not want to hear from you," Henry responded.

"Well, you knew that we needed to talk. I'm sure you received the same news that I did," Elizabeth responded.

"Yeah, and?"

"And we need to talk about this."

"Talk," Henry responded rhetorically.

"What is your problem?" Elizabeth asked.

"Well, obviously I am frustrated," Henry responded.

"Henry, you are—"

"I already know this. I got the same phone call that you did," Henry reminded Elizabeth.

"Well, this should be fairly simple. It's time to step up and be a father to Aleah," Elizabeth stated candidly.

"I will, but I will talk to you later."

"No! When will you see *your* daughter?" Elizabeth said abruptly, interrupting Henry's attempt to end the call.

"Geez, can I call you back and let you know?" Henry asked.

"Yeah, but make sure you call back," Elizabeth said.

"I will," Henry responded before hanging up the phone. They hung up.

Much to Elizabeth's surprise, Aleah was within earshot. So it was of no surprise to Elizabeth that her daughter had questions.

"Who was that, Mommy?" Aleah said in broken eighteen-month-old language.

"That was one of Mommy's friends."

"Oh! What's he name?"

"His name is…oh, do not worry, my child. You will meet him soon."

"Yay!" Aleah smiled.

In his apartment, Henry was having a different kind of conversation. He invited a friend over because he really needed to talk.

"I cannot believe I did not strap up, wear a rubber, you know."

"Hey, man, we all make mistakes," Henry's male friend replied.

"Yeah, but having a kid is like catching HIV. It never goes away, and just cost you more money the longer it lives," Henry said as he sat on the opposite side of the kitchen table.

The silence revealed the depths of Henry's offense.

His friend Jeremy finally broke the silence. "Dude, I'm a father, and the two should never be compared. Children bring so much joy. Children are not meant to be the subsequent cause of death but rather the reason for unexplainable joy."

"Wow, bro, that's a good point," Henry said, commending Jeremy for his intelligence.

"Henry, please just think about what it truly means to be a father. Do not be another deadbeat dad that donates his sperm but is not a vital part of his child's life. Be the example she needs in her life."

"I do not know if I am really ready for all of that! I will give thought to the true meaning of fatherhood, though," Henry replied.

"Uh, news flash, you're a father, so you have no choice but to get ready," Jeremy spoke in a matter-of-fact manner.

"I will try, man," Henry responded.

"She needs you. You have to do more than just try—you've got to succeed."

"All I can do is my best," Henry said, frustrated.

"But if your best is not enough, then society will reap the consequences of your failure as a parent."

"No pressure at all." Henry smirked as he sarcastically spoke.

"All right, I'll back off a little." Jeremy laughed at how flustered he'd caused Henry to become. "What's her name?"

"Aleah. Her name is Aleah," Henry answered.

"Aleah, huh?" Jeremy asked.

"Yeah."

"Well, do not let her down, my friend. Time is not something you can ever get back." Jeremy said.

"This just all seems like way too much," Henry responded.

"Then keep it in your pants. You know I am blunt with you."

"Yes, you always have been since we met in gym class in the tenth grade."

"Ha-ha. So since you decided to have sex and the result of that decision was a child, you need to realize that every moment is precious. Make every moment count," Jeremy said, offering his advice.

Make every moment count? Henry said to himself. That statement would forever be with him.

The two friends said their good-byes. Henry thanked his friend of eight years. His friend Jeremy left. Now all Henry was left with were his thoughts. He knew what he had to do, but he just wasn't ready. Several days passed by, and with each passing day, there came about another lost moment.

There are moments in life when random things radiate substantial meaning. On this day, Henry would find meaning and answers to questions he hated to ask—why, when, and what. "Why should I call? When should I call? And what should I say?"

Henry looked at his shirt, and he saw the illustration of a man breaking through the ground, which, for Henry, symbolized rising above circumstances and adversity. The slogan read, "Why Wait?" He looked at his favorite pair of shoes, and this particular slogan read, "Just Do It!"

It was there, in that moment, the most random of things turned the lightbulb on in Henry's mind. He reached for his phone.

18

Elizabeth was particularly busy one Saturday morning in March. Much to her surprise, the phone began to ring.

"Henry?" Elizabeth was excited but also beginning to feel overwhelmed.

The phone call only added to her mounting stress. Aleah was running like a track star and falling everywhere imaginable. Elizabeth had yet to shower, her hair was wild and awry from the rough night's sleep she'd had, and her eyes wore bags from periodically having to wake up throughout the night. In her opinion, her clothes were raggedy, and she just wanted to lie down so she could sleep for an uninterrupted eight hours.

"Hello?" Elizabeth finally responded.

"About time! What took you so long to answer?" Henry asked.

"Henry, you have no idea what I've been through this morning. You finally decide to call and just assume I am sitting by the phone waiting for your call?"

"Actually, I am only calling to speak to Aleah," Henry responded rather candidly.

"Hold up." Elizabeth held the phone up and called for Aleah to come.

Aleah ran toward her mommy and reached for the phone.

Elizabeth pulled away. "Hey do you know who is on the phone?"

"Gimme, Mommy, gimme," Aleah said excitedly.

Elizabeth did not have the energy to fight. "Here."

"Hi, Aleah," Henry said.

"Who's this?" Aleah asked.

"Your daddy," Henry said with as much excitement as possible.

Aleah giggled. "My dada?"

"Yes, Aleah," Henry said, reiterating who he was.

"Here, Mommy." The one-and-a-half-year-old Aleah handed the phone back and ran back to the playroom.

"Hello?" Elizabeth said as she got back on the phone.

"Hey, so when can I see her?" Henry asked.

"When would you like to?" Elizabeth responded.

"I really wish you would not answer a question with a question, but anyway, how's next Friday?"

"How about next Saturday?" Elizabeth asked.

"Okay, what about three in the afternoon?" Henry replied.

"That will be fine," Elizabeth responded.

"Where would you like to meet at?" Henry asked.

"You can just come by my house."

"Okay, I will see you then," Henry replied.

Aleah ran around the playroom without a care in the world. Elizabeth looked in and reveled at the life God had blessed her with. Aleah turned around as if she'd been listening to the entire phone conversation and asked, "When is Daddy coming?"

19

The day had come. Elizabeth dressed Aleah in her best dress and did her hair flawlessly. She was meeting her dad for the first time, and Elizabeth wanted her to look her best. Beneath the surface, she wondered why she placed such high importance on Henry when he placed such little importance on them—Aleah and her. Her resolve was she loved their child and desired what was best for her.

Then 3:00 p.m. came, but Henry did not. Elizabeth gave him an additional twenty minutes before she began to worry.

"Where is Daddy at?" Aleah asked randomly as she sat at the dining room table.

"Let me find out, hon."

Elizabeth dialed Henry's number but received no answer. It was now 3:30 p.m., and there was a knock at the door. Henry stood at the door, releasing relatively empty apologies for his tardiness.

Elizabeth frowned at him. "No time for excuses."

"Who is that, Mom?"

"Aleah, this is your father."

"Who, Mommy?" Aleah asked.

"This is your dada." Elizabeth spoke in a manner that Aleah would understand.

"Hey, Aleah!"

Aleah smiled, but she didn't know what to say.

Henry smiled then pulled a teddy bear from behind his back. "Look what I have!" He smirked as he looked at Aleah, showing her the gift he'd brought for her.

"Ooooo! Yay!" Aleah said, smiling. She loved gifts.

"This is for you, baby girl."

Aleah walked toward Henry and reached for the little brown bear. Henry quickly grabbed Aleah and sat her on his lap. Aleah squirmed until both feet were on the ground. She ran back to her mom and jumped into her arms.

"Aleah, go see your daddy."

"I don't want to, Mommy," Aleah responded.

"But he came here just to see you."

"Come here, baby," Henry called.

Aleah slowly walked toward her dad. He smiled as if they'd known each other forever. Aleah felt fearful because he was a man she'd just met, yet courageous because deep inside, she knew that he was a man she was supposed to meet.

"It is so nice to meet you. I cannot wait to have a lot of fun with you and get to know more about you," Henry said.

Aleah smiled.

Henry bounced her on his leg. "We are going to go get ice cream."

"Yum! I love ice cream!" Aleah yelled.

Elizabeth's face lit up brighter than the sun shining from above.

"We are going to eat so much pizza and potato chips and play lots, I mean lots of games."

There was a slight pause in the conversation.

"You are going to have dreams about pizza. You will probably be eating and saying, 'Yummy, yummy,' in your sleep," Henry said.

"You're really silly, Dada," Aleah said.

Aleah was so excited. She'd finally met her dada, whatever that really meant. Henry was well-intentioned, but was he ready to be the father that Aleah needed? So many birthdays to come, so many memories to create, so many tears to wipe, and so many smiles to cause.

One man was God inspired to be all that Aleah could ever need. One could not be sure, but presumably, that man would give his life for hers. And another man was God designed to be her father. If such a sacrifice was required, could that man give his life for hers? If his death was the only way to save her life, would he give his life for hers?

20

O n the other side of the city, Elizabeth lamented while thinking of her favorite girl, Aleah.

She remembered how amazing Shay had been, talking to Aleah while she was still in the womb and replacing much of what a father was supposed to be.

"I want to see Shay!" toddler Aleah would say.

Aleah seemed to spend more time at Shay's house than she did at mine, Elizabeth thought.

She wiped her tears then continued to weep about the possibility of losing her only child if she does not receive a new heart. She wanted someone to be angry at, but the only person that came to mind was the kidnapper who now lay in the hospital fighting for his life.

As Aleah had aged, Elizabeth had been full of joy at her developing personality. She had been a little sass with a lot of sweet. She had been a little funk with much spunk.

To Elizabeth, her mother, she was the apple of her eye. *How do you replace the loss of a child?* Elizabeth thought. Her answer was swift and direct: *You don't.* She made haste conclusions because she couldn't bear such a surprise if Aleah did not receive a heart before it was too late.

Her thoughts ran a marathon in minutes. She wanted them to slow down or, even better, to just stop. Even if for just a short while, peace of mind would be priceless. She'd lost the person who meant the most to her. She was alone in the dark and dismal place she once called home. The place she'd once called home had now become a dreadful, horrid abode that she hated to return to.

Elizabeth walked from the living room to Aleah's room. It was there that her depression deepened. She looked at the murals on the wall and remembered how much Aleah loved all the Disney princesses and more so herself. The photos on the wall told a million stories. Stories filled with joy. Stories filled with love and hope for a beautiful tomorrow. It was the story of a life that now faced death because unprecedented evil lurked and loitered everywhere imaginable.

Elizabeth cried for many reasons, some of which she couldn't fully understand. She wasn't ready to live life without her daughter. She simply had no idea how to do that—how could she possibly cope? Only one idea came to mind.

21

—〰—

S hay was startled by the knocking at the door.

"It's 10:03 p.m. Who is here? I am sure I made no arrangements for guests," Shay said aloud, though no one was listening.

Shay looked through the peephole, and much to his surprise, Elizabeth was standing outside his door. Her shirt was drenched from the tears she'd cried. The bags underneath her eyes served as the evidence of little sleep and persistent waterworks.

"Well, can I come in?" Elizabeth asked, making an attempt at humor.

"Oh yeah, you definitely can," Shay responded quickly as he opened the door.

"So how are you?" Elizabeth asked.

"Not so well, but doing all that I can to get better."

Elizabeth choked back tears during the brief silence.

"But, hey, how are you?" Shay asked.

Elizabeth looked at Shay with a deer-in-the-headlights sort of look.

"Don't answer," Shay said as he wiped away her tears.

Then the two of engaged in a much-needed embrace.

Shay began tapping his foot and scratching his head.

"What's on your mind, Shay?" Elizabeth asked.

"I have to do something," Shay responded.

"Shay, you are so sweet, but there is nothing that you can do."

"I will go see the director first thing in the morning."

"Shay, what will that do?"

"Maybe they will have a heart for her." Shay began to cry.

"Shay, thank you so much," Elizabeth said.

"I will not stand for it," Shay said sternly.

"You're not God. You do not get to fight with death. Death always wins. Yep, eventually death will win every time, and with everyone."

"Oh my gosh, will you stop with your defeatist attitude?" Shay banged his hand on the table.

"I've never seen you get this mad, Shay. Stop it!"

"No, because I am the only person that believes in the power of love around here," Shay said.

"You're not the only person. It's just that my sweet baby girl lay fighting for her life, and unless God himself provides a miracle, we will be burying her, and she will be nothing more than a memory," Elizabeth said.

"She's not going in the ground. I cannot…we cannot handle that," Shay said with assurance.

"Shay…oh, Shay. You're in denial. Please stop," Elizabeth responded.

"I'm going to do something. Watch." Shay nodded as he made his seemingly empty declaration.

"Okay, Shay, okay," Elizabeth said with cynicism and impatience in her voice.

Elizabeth and Shay talked from dusk till dawn. They encouraged each other and felt revitalized from the positive energy in the living room. Elizabeth smiled because she knew that she could always count on Shay. The two traded tears and told memorable stories about Aleah. The idea of her life ending was beyond belief. Something inside of Shay caused him to only partially grasp the reality of what was upon Elizabeth and him.

There was something so special about this man. *Who loves a child the way he does? It's special because there's no biological connection. He goes out of his way to comfort me. Even when there remains no hope, he's hopeful that he'll somehow save the life of my little baby girl.*

Elizabeth began to cry, and as Shay went to wipe Elizabeth's tears, she laid in his arms. Shay stroked her hair and rubbed her back. Elizabeth leaned in closer then looked up at Shay. Eventually, their eyes met, and love consumed the moment.

In that very moment, Elizabeth wanted to be nowhere else besides right there in Shay's arms, and Shay did not desire anyone else to lie in his arms, gaze into his eyes, or lean into his heart besides Elizabeth Prim.

Elizabeth closed her eyes, and Shay pulled her closer. Their lips touched for the first time in the history of their friendship, and magic captured the moment.

"I love you," Elizabeth said.

"I love you too," Shay responded as he laid Elizabeth down on the couch.

Their hands moved about, but both quickly pulled their hands away.

Shay rubbed his hands down Elizabeth's body, and his brain connected with the curvature of her hips. It felt so good to be touched in such a way, Elizabeth could not deny. She took Shay's hands and held them close. They stared into each other's eyes and contemplated the ensuing moment.

Then like an unfortunate reminder, the sound of the crash vividly replayed in his mind. He jumped back. "We have to stop. This is not right." He paused.

"It's perfect, Shay!"

For a moment, the effect of their grief escaped into the deepest section of their souls.

He stood up and paced the room. Elizabeth watched without a clue of how to help. She just wanted to, for just a moment, forget the reality of her present world. She just wanted Shay to love her, to touch her, and to help her escape momentarily to a different place. A place where pain no longer exists.

The words Shay would speak next would, for a long time, confuse Elizabeth.

"I'm her...her keeper. I am her..." Shay paused. "I am her soul keeper!" He closed his eyes, nodded, and smiled as he continued revealing the epiphany he recently discovered.

Elizabeth was perplexed as she asked, "What?"

22

—m—

The two of them, Elizabeth and Shay, awoke with no regrets. They laughed about the obvious that would continue to be ignored—love! They loved each other, but love could not have its way. Both Elizabeth and Shay had a greater focus, one dealing with grief and loss and the other confronting death and hope.

"Thank you for staying, Liz, but I must kick you out now." Shay laughed.

"Oh, I see how it is." Elizabeth reciprocated the laughter.

They went back to their respective lives. They were connected in so many ways yet disconnected just the same. Elizabeth made her way home, and Shay got ready to go to the hospital.

Shay now stood at the place he'd begged for life once before.

"I knew you'd be returning," the director said.

"I didn't have a choice," Shay replied.

"Oh, Shay, we always have a choice," the director replied.

"Okay, Doc, so what's going on?" Shay asked.

"What do you mean?" Doc replied.

"Do you have a heart for Aleah?"

"I am really sorry, I do not, and those people in black are awaiting her death."

"The people in black?" Shay asked.

"Oh, sorry, the coroners that will transport her body to her next waiting place if she does indeed die."

"What place is this?" Shay asked.

"The morgue. There she will await burial," the director candidly responded.

"I will not let them have her," Shay declared.

@@@"What would be the reason for keeping her body?" Doc asked.

"Her soul, Doc! I can restore her soul," Shay responded.

"I'm not sure how you could do that. Listen, Shay, your only hope is prayer and that depends on if God is feeling gracious and merciful. Sometimes, justice and swift conclusion is his default."

"Hey, how do you even know that God is a he?" Shay asked.

"Maybe I don't." The director quickly concluded the ensuing conversation.

Shay turned within and began to pray. "Dear God, if you are real, I need you to show me. I am earnestly asking that you save the life of my godchild, Aleah. There is nothing that is too hard for you. I've read your Bible countless times and it says that nothing is impossible to those that believe. God, my faith is strong, so my hope is that you are true to your word. I need you, God. I really do. I will do whatever I have to do, but God, I hope you do your part as well!"

On the other side of the city the People in Black prepared themselves to gather the next client's body to transport it to its next destination.

"So it looks like we will have another casualty," one worker, Baxter, said.

"Casualty? It's not like she was at war," the other worker, Trolley, replied.

"Every soul is at war until death has its victory," Baxter contested Trolley's statement.

"So what will be the cause of death for this one anyway? I'm sorry, let me be more clear, this 'casualty'?" Trolley laughed as he teased Baxter.

"Watch your mouth, Trolley! I think it was a car accident of some sort."

"How old is she?" Trolley asked.

"You know I'm not sure, Trolley!" Baxter replied.

"She is five, Trolley, five!" the boss replied.

"Thanks, boss!" Trolley replied.

The boss gave the look of approval for Trolley's appropriate use of manners.

"Oh yeah, the boss knows everything!" Baxter replied with a small dose of sarcasm.

"Yeah, you're actually right for once, Baxter, the boss does know everything," Trolley replied.

"Okay, Trolley, I think your nose is a little brown." Baxter laughed at his joke.

"Okay, shut your filthy mouths, especially you, Baxter, and do what you need to do so we can get going. You guys, both of you are really pissing me off!" the boss said.

"Geez, what's gotten into him?" Baxter asked.

"I can hear you, Baxter. Shut your mouth before I send you home…forever."

A peculiar silence fell over the room.

"Make yourselves useful. Go check the car to make sure that we have everything that we need for our next job. Then meet me right back here in this room."

"Okay, boss!" Trolley replied.

"Thank you, Trolley, my good worker!" The boss offered accolades to one of his two workers.

What a flipping brownnoser! Baxter thought of Trolley.

Baxter and Trolley checked the car then returned to the room where they were expected to meet the boss. "All is well?" boss asked.

"Yes, boss, yes!" Trolley replied.

"Wow, Trolley…" Baxter began.

"What is it now, Baxter?" Trolley asked.

"Why are you such a suck-up to the boss?" Baxter asked.

"Why are you even concerned about it, Baxter?" Trolley responded as he began walking toward Baxter.

"You want to test me, Trolley?" Baxter asked as he inched closer to Trolley as well.

"It's beyond time for me to kick your arrogant and rude ass."

"Then do something about it!" Baxter said as he and Trolley now stood face to face.

"Enough! I swear, you both better get back to work, and I mean now. I swear that I will beat the living daylights out of both of your sorry asses."

Baxter and Trolley walked away as they figured it would be a bad idea to upset the boss any more than they already did.

Baxter cleared off the table where the body of the newly deceased would lay. Trolley searched for a while to find a bed and room small enough to accommodate the minute size of the little girl who is sure to die.

"Boss, why is it always so hot in here?" Baxter asked as he wiped sweat from his forehead.

"Geez, I do not know Baxter—maybe you should brush your teeth a little more often."

"You know, boss, you're kind of…" Baxter began saying.

The boss quickly rose to his feet and began walking toward Baxter, "I am what? What, Baxter?" The boss ground his teeth and clenched his fists. "I will knock you right out, Baxter!" The boss said sternly.

"Calm down, boss!" Baxter said with immense fear.

"What am I, Baxter?" The boss slapped Baxter in the head.

Baxter rose to his feet. "All right, boss, you're taking it too far now."

"Oh, am I?" The boss grabbed Baxter around the neck and squeezed until Baxter fell to the floor.

Trolley's jaws hung as far open as possible.

"All right, boss, all right!" Baxter said in embarrassment and desperation.

The mood finally eased up. The boss, Baxter, and Trolley labored to ready the room for the newly deceased.

"Hey, boss, when is the funeral for this little girl?"

"I do not know, and fortunately, I do not care."

"Okay!" Trolley did not want get beat down like Baxter did earlier in the day.

The sun began to fade and night made its way in. The boss liked to work in the dark.

"It's time!" the boss said.

The team gathered their tools—gavel, hammer, and leather straps, coats with the special hood, masks—just in case—shoes to trudge the mud, and the item the boss grabbed that shocked other team members, a sword.

"Boss, a sword?" Baxter asked.

"Darn it, Baxter! You just never know what can happen!" the boss replied.

"Oh yeah, boss. Yeah, you're right, boss," Baxter quickly agreed.

"I am always right, Baxter. Now, for once, shut your darn mouth and let's go."

The team was off to gather the body of the newly deceased.

23

Shay prayed with all his might in hopes for a miracle. "God, you said that perfect love casts out all fear. Then why am I afraid? You said that you hold the keys to death and the grave! If that's true, then why is death the victor and the grave succeeding?"

Doc leaned in and listened more closely at how wonderfully Shay beckoned God.

"You say that you can do all things. I've always believed that you could…"

The director smiled.

"Well now, I need you. I need you to reward me for overcoming this grave test of my faith. I love you, I need you, and Aleah needs you. Please save her, God. Once more, God, I need you to take the keys from death and impede the grave. I do not want to lose her…"

The director and his wife stood on their feet.

"I command your blessings, God. I command your blessings, God. Right now, God. Right now! God, I need you. I need you, God. You're the God of second chances. So dear Heavenly Father, Aleah needs a second chance now…"

Now a few more gathered around. "Keep praying, Shay. Do not open your eyes. God hears your every prayer. Who are we to question the sovereignty and miracle-working power of God? I hear him saying that you are not alone and that he will fight your battles. He is faithful. Do not give up the faith, Shay," Doc encouraged Shay.

The rest of the staff who were present looked at their director with disbelief and curiosity.

"God, please fight my battles." Shay began to weep uncontrollably. "Please fight my battles, God. I do not want to lose her, and she doesn't deserve to die, dear Lord, but my gracious Heavenly Father, your will be done!" Shay kept his eyes closed and silently revered the greatness of God.

"Hey, guys, let's go," Doc said.

"All right!" the staff replied.

"Actually, hold up. Let me make a phone call!" Doc suddenly said.

The people in black sat in their black, tinted SUV when suddenly the phone began to ring. "Who could possibly be calling me?" Luke, the boss of the People in Black Unit said.

"Hello, Luke!" the director said.

"Hey! What is it, Mr. Director?"

"I need you to wait on the body of Aleah. We will call once we've made a decision," the director replied.

"Um, what are you talking about? We are already on the way!" Luke yelled as he motioned for Baxter to put the SUV in drive.

"Then we will stop you at the door."

"No, you will not. We have a quota to meet for this quarter, so get off of my phone and out of my way," Luke responded firmly.

"Okay, I am not going to argue with you. I am your director too," the director reminded Luke. "She is not deceased just yet, and the body is not ready."

"I have my own business, man!" Luke, in return, reminded the director.

"Which would not be a business if I didn't sign the contract." The director attempted to highlight the reality of their business relationship.

"Oops, ya signed it, Doc!" Luke said sarcastically.

"Did you forget that it's 100 percent revocable? So you may not want to come for the body if you're being told not to."

"Well, Doc, I am not in the mood to take orders, so I am coming!" Luke said in a very matter-of-fact manner.

"So be it! I'll be waiting. What a sad song you'll be singing, Luke!" The director delivered his resolve.

"Screw you, Doc. I'll see you soon."

The director turned to the team. "Please grab my binder with all of the contracts for Dark City Suites."

"All right, Mr. Director!" Mitch replied.

"Will you also get the blue bag?" the director asked.

"What's in there, hon?" Mona asked.

"I'm afraid you do not want to know."

The director and the crew stood at the gate, awaiting the arrival of the People in Black. Moments later a black SUV with tinted windows pulled up. Baxter lowered all the windows. Luke smiled, "You ready, Mr. Director?" he asked.

Elsewhere in the city, Elizabeth did the best that she could to plan Aleah's funeral. She cried through the conversations, but she wanted to be prepared for the worst.

24

———∽∞∽———

"Hello, you have reached Monuments Best, this is Halle. How may we assist you today?" the receptionist greeted.

"Hi, I would like to get a quote for a monument for a five-year-old girl," Elizabeth responded somberly.

"Oh, how sad. I am so sorry to hear that. Give me just a moment," Halle responded with much empathy.

While waiting the return of the receptionist, Elizabeth browsed other resources online and searched for burial costs and services. "I really need a place for the call…"

"Okay, I am back, ma'am!" Halle interrupted.

"Thank you. So how much?" Elizabeth asked.

"So your total cost will be $250.00 plus tax," Halle answered.

"All right, thank you. I will make some more calls to compare prices. I will most likely be purchasing the monument from Monuments Best though," Elizabeth said.

"No problem, ma'am. We will be looking forward to hearing from you."

Shay continued praying for God's blessing and much-needed miracle.

Elizabeth called Shay for his input regarding funeral processions and a tombstone for Aleah. "Shay usually answers his phone. Eh, maybe he will call back though!"

Elizabeth called five more places regarding Aleah's tombstone; she compared prices, styles, and thought about what her little Aleah would like. The emotions were too much. She presumed she'd feel a sense of joy because she'd done something in Aleah's honor, but her perceived strength was far less than she understood at the time she took on this daunting task.

She dialed the strange area code. Her parents had moved to North Carolina, which is where they always dreamed of retiring. "Mom!" Elizabeth said after hearing her mother's voice.

"Elizabeth!" Her mother, Mrs. Prim, responded.

"Mom, I just cannot do it!" Elizabeth said through her tears.

"Your dad and I are already on our way to New York. We knew our little girl would need her parents at a time like this," Mrs. Prim responded.

"Thanks, Mom. I am trying to plan the funeral, but there is no way that I can keep it together long enough."

"Darling, she is not dead."

Elizabeth paused, but was at a loss for words.

"We love you, and don't you ever forget that, Liz!" her mother said.

"I love you guys too," Elizabeth responded.

"We'll see you soon, baby," her dad said over the bluetooth. "Thank you, guys. I will see you soon," Elizabeth responded.

Elizabeth hung up the phone. She cried uncontrollably. She cleaned her house spotless, but Aleah's room remained the same. She laid in Aleah's Doc McStuffins bed and clenched Aleah's favorite stuffed animal tight. She remembered the moments when she held her little girl just as tight. She yelled like a woman scorned. She wanted to fight death and the grave herself, but the reality was that tears could be her only recompense. She looked at Aleah's pink-accented wall and saw the purple princess dress hanging up from her fifth birthday party. The pictures surrounding the dress pushed to the surface memories too difficult to bear. *I could lay here forever! I could die right here,* she thought. She remembered the way Aleah caught the little frogs that hopped; how she held them with such tender care and the way she kissed them with such little-girl joy. The moment was akin to a true tale of the princess and the frog. *What a sweet little girl!* Elizabeth thought. She smiled when she thought of how Aleah rode the ponies for the first time. She was 100 percent delighted in her memories of Aleah. Now euphoria had turned to an unexplainable sadness that pierced the heart unto death. "I could die right here...right now!" she said with such commitment and surety.

Her parents were approximately three hours away. "I need you guys to hurry." Elizabeth wept as she recognized her apparent deepening depression. Anguish took her captive—mind, body, and soul. The agony felt was akin to death and at best rest was the only solution for sanity.

She opened her eyes and reality sat upon her like no other time than now.

25

—⚬—

The director remained puzzled at the fight that was ensuing. It grew increasingly dark at an unexpected rate of speed.

The director looked at Luke and shook his head. "What a challenge this guy will be!" he said sarcastically.

"Okay, Doc, get out of the way," Luke demanded.

"Luke, take your crew and go," the director replied.

Meanwhile, Shay continued praying as powerfully as he could.

What the director didn't know was that Luke had already sent an impostor for the body. During their exchange of unpleasant words, which lead to no agreed-upon solution, the impostor came out with the body. His eyes were red as blood and his smile as crooked as the Joker's. "We're ready, Luke!" the impostor said.

Luke smiled. "Looks like I win after all."

"Not so fast, Luke!" the director replied.

The primary problem of the People in Black and their impostor was that the getaway vehicle was on the other side of the director and his team, and Luke's crew were not all able to fit into the SUV which was parked in a different area than the getaway vehicle.

"Toss me my blue bag, Mona," the director said.

The director caught the bag and his team marveled at the samurai swords that were revealed. "Time for battle, guys."

The fight of their lives began. The thunder roared and the rain cried out for mercy as Mona wept. There was no peace, only chaos. Shay prayed harder and the earth shook, the waters rumbled, and darkness fell upon the earth. Aleah's body floated through the air with both sides trying to catch her. The dark side met with good and this was war. The sun hid its face and darkness consumed the day.

Doc was quite skilled with the sword. One by one, members of the Dark City Suites/the People in Black team fell. Luke had powers akin to magic. Some had called Luke the devil himself, but Doc…the director had another name. They called him savior, healer, defender—God!

The harder Shay prayed, the harder the director's team fought. Shay opened his eyes. He looked through his body and observed the chaos going on in the parking lot. It was literally Hell on earth. He ran outside. He wanted to help, but this seemed somewhat out of his realm of expertise. He wasn't sure his skill set would stand a chance against such talented fighters, but then he saw the girl that made his blood run—Aleah.

He ran toward the scene. He saw one beheaded and another bleeding to death. He saw a sword through the neck of the red-eyed man with the black coat. Luke was escaping as the director and his team continued trying to fight their way to the body.

The director sensed a lack of faith elsewhere in the universe and well, as stated earlier—faith compels. The team grew weaker as faith waned though Shay was not encouraged nor was he discouraged by faith or the lack thereof. He leaped and while in the air, grabbed a sword that Mona threw at him. *Is this a movie or book?* he thought. "This is insane, but anything for Aleah!"

Luke dropped the body. "I've waited for you. For days, I've known that you'd be the one I'd have to defeat in order to further my establishment and finish this job."

"Over my dead body, literally, and I do mean literally over my dead body!"

Shay had never seen such evil. If evil had a face, it was the face presently glaring at Shay. If evil had a name it had to be Luke. He looked at Shay, and if looks truly could kill, Luke would have succeeded in committing murder that very moment. Shay would be dead and Aleah gone forever. "My life for hers, if necessary!"

"So be it…" Luke said as he swung two swords across, each other toward Shay's face.

Shay ducked and stabbed at Luke's leg. "There is no fear of death here!" Shay smiled. He was born for a moment such as this.

Luke stabbed toward Shay's back. "But there is death in fear. You will fear me and that will lead to your demise," Luke declared.

The sky was red, with minimal sun on one side and total blackness on the other. The universe revealed ambiguity and neutrality and confusion of sorts concerning the situation at hand. The clouds moved rapidly and the rain repeatedly wet the pavement.

Love compels! Shay thought. Shay looked at Aleah's nearly lifeless body. "Love compels!"

Luke kicked Shay in the stomach. Shay stumbled back then roundhouse-kicked Luke in the head. Luke stepped back and struck Shay in the side of the head with the butt of his sword. Shay fell down but rose right back to his feet.

"Is that all you got for me?" Shay asked cynically.

"You'd be surprised at what's coming for you," Luke replied.

Shay kept as close an eye on the little girl as he could. Doc and his team continued battling the People in Black from the Dark City Suites.

Shay dropped his sword then Luke dropped his. It was time for a good ole-fashioned fistfight. "Time to regurgitate those boxing skills!" Shay said to himself.

Shay squared his feet, raised his hands then clenched his fists. "Come on!" he challenged Luke.

Luke smiled. "Gladly!"

Shay moved around and attempted to calculate Luke's first move.

Luke looked down and then back up.

Shay's eyes had a burning like never seen before.

Luke swung and Shay dodged. Shay hit Luke with a right hook then a left hook, an uppercut with the right hand then two jabs with the left hand. Luke stumbled. "Ha! You fool!" Luke said as he reached for his sword. Luke kicked Shay in the head instead.

Shay fell down and lay in a state of near-unconsciousness and he heard, "Shay...get up, Uncle Shay! You got to get up!" It was the voice of little Journey.

Luke assumed that the victory was his though he wanted to seal the deal with the heart of his contender. He walked over and grabbed his sword. Like a flash of lightning, Shay snapped back.

Luke was stunned as Shay kicked the sword out of his hand then roundhouse-kicked him in the side of the head. After that, Shay released a flurry of punches.

Luke ducked down and grabbed his sword. Shay back-pedalled toward his sword. Shay quickly picked up his sword then their blades met. Luke pierced Shay's side and slammed a crown of thorns on his head. Shay stumbled back as Luke spat in his face. Shay looked down at Aleah then at the director. Aleah's need for him and the director's approval of his ability to finish what he'd started was all the motivation he needed. The director nodded his head, "The time is now Shay—it's now or never, but you can do it."

Shay cut Luke across his left leg, then his right leg, his left arm then the right. Luke cut the side of Shay's neck, but Shay pierced his.

The earth shook then stopped. Total blackness fell upon the face of the earth then the sun began brightly shining.

Shay fell on top of Aleah's body. "I love you!"

The director's phone began to ring!

"Hello…"

26

—∿—

Elizabeth sat up in Aleah's bed. The time had come to embrace the reality that consumed her life. She stretched out and yawned. No more tears would come. She dialed her parents' phone number, but they did not answer. She called Shay, but he didn't respond. She considered calling Henry, but resolved her consideration to the fact that he was a lowlife who would be of no help whatsoever. She was ready to deal with her anguish and agony once and for all. She looked at her Bible then threw it against the wall. She then picked it up and placed it neatly in her fireplace and said, "A loving God would not let my little girl die." God wanted to speak, but he was especially busy at this time of day.

She laid a picture of her and Aleah on the bed where she last laid. She kissed Aleah's pictures good-bye then walked out of her room. She was hungry but only a little. She ran her fingers through her hair, looked at her phone then walked into the kitchen. The sun was beginning to set, and the rain began profusely pouring. As she walked out, her parents began calling, but she'd forgotten that the phone was on vibrate and did not hear the call. They were less than an hour away now. She grabbed the knife and laid it on the counter. She took two onions and one bell pepper. She casually chopped but eventually the intensity with which she chopped increased. She began to weep then she put the knife to her neck. "I can't live without you, baby." She tried to stop crying and comfort herself. "There are other reasons to live," she reasoned.

Her parents called again. "Why isn't Lizzie answering the phone?" they began to worry.

"No! No! No! No!" She didn't want to die, but it was too hard living. "No! You cannot be serious, Elizabeth." The second person, self-serving, self-narrative conversation began. "You are better than this…" She paused. "But without Aleah you are incomplete." The pain escalated and the knife excavated her flesh. She pressed it hard into her neck then released it. "Where's your phone, Elizabeth?" She paced the kitchen. "Forget the phone!" She walked into Aleah's bedroom. She looked around one last time. She saw her phone lying on the bed. She walked toward it but changed her mind. "I will not live without you."

She laid down, back first, onto Aleah's bed. She looked at their picture and wept. "You gotta do it, Lizzie." Then it happened—she pressed the knife into her neck. She slowly slid it across until she gasped for air, dropping the knife to the floor. As she lay there taking her final breaths, her phone began to vibrate. She looked at the name which read My Hero!

27

Elizabeth's mom was becoming increasingly worried because her daughter was not answering the phone. It wasn't like Elizabeth to fail to answer as many times as she did today. They were less than thirty minutes away and naturally anxiety increased. "I am going to call 911!" Mrs. Prim said.

"Are you sure you want to do that, hon?" Mr. Prim asked.

"I'd rather follow my intuition—my gut feeling, sweetie, than failing to make the call for fear of upsetting her and regretting it later," Mrs. Prim responded.

"All right, well I trust you and, yes, Elaine, better to be safe than sorry."

Elaine began dialing 911. Her hands shook from the fear that consumed her. She couldn't put her finger on it, but something was horrifically wrong with Elizabeth.

"911, what is your emergency?" the dispatch representative asked.

"It is my daughter, Elizabeth. I think something may be wrong," Mrs. Prim responded.

"Why do you think that, ma'am?" the representative asked.

"She's not answering her phone, and she's under a lot of stress currently."

"There could be a lot of reasons that people do not answer their phone."

"Please go check on her," Mrs. Prim said with an extreme amount of desperation.

"Address, please," the 911 dispatch responded.

"Her address is 89 Summer Lane," Mrs. Prim responded.

"Okay, I am dispatching an emergency response team now," the representative assured.

They disconnected the phone call. Elaine and Roger sat in silence for the rest of the ride to Elizabeth's house. The atmosphere inside of the car was tense, stagnant, and gloomy. Both Elaine and Roger—Mr. and Mrs. Prim hoped for the best, but they understood that the worst was possible.

The emergency response team quickly gathered necessary equipment and hurried to their vehicle. Three minutes went by and they now arrived at 89 Summer Lane. They circled the necessary areas of the house then knocked on the door.

"Hey, is anyone home?" one of the paramedics asked.

They received no response. Elizabeth, in her state of near-unconsciousness, faintly heard the knocking. "Hu…" Elizabeth tried to speak, but she'd lost too much blood to verbally communicate loud enough for anyone to hear her even if they were within earshot. Silently, she prayed, but she'd lost both hope for survival and desire to live. Death's dilemma presented Elizabeth with one of her greatest challenges—die without dignity or live without love. Aleah was one of the key reasons that Elizabeth felt loved. *What would I be living for?* she asked her disintegrating mind. *Who would I be living for?* she thought, forgetting that two people who loved her dearly were near. *Who would have ever thought that dying was easier than living?* she asked herself as she closed her eyes, attempted to smile, and began relinquishing her will to fight for something she'd come to appreciate—life! All of her will to live faded into a place remarkably unexplainable. From deep inside, her soul wept. From the outside-in, Elizabeth stained crimson forever. Forever she would love Aleah, and forever Aleah would live on in her heart and mind, but forever itself had now surfaced as an anomaly. *What does forever really look like on the other side of life?*

One of the paramedics looked into the window and much to his surprise, he saw the wretched scene of a young woman presumably deceased. "Let's go, guys!" He ran around to the front door and went to open it. "Stop!" his coworker said. "We cannot go in there before the police come!"

"I do not care about policy right now. I am going in any way! I'm guessing that her life is more important than policy," the paramedic said.

"Hey, man, it's your job."

Another car pulled up. Elizabeth heard all as she gracefully fell to her demise. She heard other random noises, but none aiding her rescue. She elegantly expired. The last thing she heard was, "That's my baby in there…"

What she didn't hear was the door being kicked open by her father and the sirens loudly sounding near her house.

The floor was stained red as was Aleah's bed. Mr. and Mrs. Prim ran like track stars to Elizabeth's side. "Not my baby!" they yelled as both wailed the cry none would ever forget.

Paramedics did their best to calm Elizabeth's parents while they performed resuscitation techniques.

The officers assessed the environment. They quickly ruled out robbery as a motive. One officer saw the knife on the floor and moved toward the conclusion of suicide.

Paramedics worked hard to find a pulse. Mrs. Prim cried the saddest cry ever heard by those around her. Mr. Prim demonstrated pain incomparable to what these professionals had ever witnessed.

The officers encouraged Mr. and Mrs. Prim to speak with them when they were calm enough to do so. The officers eventually got the information they needed in spite of the emotional pain being expressed by both parents. The information was transcribed by the officer as follows:

Officer: When was the last time you saw your daughter?

Mr. Prim: We saw her approximately three months ago.

Officer: If you do not mind me asking, why so long?

Mrs. Prim: Well we have been living in North Carolina.

Officer: Okay, well that makes perfect sense!

Officer: Has Elizabeth ever given you any reason to believe that she would hurt herself?

Mr. Prim: No, she has always handled life pretty responsibly.

Officer: Sir, ma'am, I have to ask, what do you think caused this to happen?

Mrs. Prim: She recently lost a child…

The officers took notes and continued assessing the scene. The rest of the conversation was about verifying details and clarifying previously stated information.

The paramedics performed their procedures and rushed the body to the van. Mr. Prim followed behind with the car while Mrs. Prim held Elizabeth's hand on the way to the hospital. She believed the power of love to be an instrument of healing. She spoke encouraging and kind words to Elizabeth. She spoke living words to a dying soul. Many of her latter statements began with, "If you ever need me…" and ended with, "I will always love you."

The van finally arrived. They rushed Elizabeth to the nearest room. Ironically, her room was two doors from Aleah's.

"Life support?" The doctors looked at each other.

"Possibly!" one doctor replied.

28

"I am looking for the director," the representative said.

"Speaking! Who is this?" the director replied.

"This is Aliana from the Heart to Heart Association," the receptionist said.

"It couldn't be…" Doc said, puzzled.

"We just had a young woman arrive. She lost a lot of blood, and we do not think she will make it," Aliana said.

"Well what's the situation?" Doc asked.

"She's on life support, but honestly, it doesn't look promising," Aliana replied with sadness defining her tone.

"We will take the heart. It's our only glimmer of hope at this point. I'm not sure how to say this, but…hurry?" the director replied.

"We will do what we can, sir!" Aliana replied.

The director was somewhat enamored by the power of love. He looked at Shay. The director was so proud of the faith of this young man. Shay's prayers continued to hit Heaven's door until it opens.

"Dear God, come now, bring your blessing now, we need your miracle-working power to prove itself once…" Shay continued.

"You can stop praying now," the black guard said as she flung the door open.

"Why did you interrupt me? And where am I?" Shay asked.

"You're in my office, Shay!" the director replied.

"This feels like the most eventful dream ever," Shay informed the director and the others who were present.

"Well hold on because your life just got more eventful," the director said.

"Not sure how that could be because the dream was literally something you'd read in a book or watch in a movie," Shay responded.

"Shay, we have some news for you…" Doc said.

"I hope it is good, Doc, because I cannot stand any more bad news," Shay replied.

"You might want to take a seat."

"It's that serious?" Shay asked.

"Possibly, Shay, it is that serious," Doc replied.

"Okay, Doc, do not keep me in suspense," Shay said quickly.

"I think we may have a heart," the director delivered the news with very little emotion, but his smile convinced every one of his pure joy.

Shay allowed the silence its due time. Then he remembered the fight and wondered if it was really just a dream. "Well that is so awesome, Doc. When will we know?" Shay asked.

"In approximately thirty minutes to an hour." The director nodded his head while smiling.

The hospital had done all they could to save the young woman's life, but the time came when they pulled life support away.

One of the first calls was to the director, "Hello, may we speak to the director?" Aliana asked.

"This is him," the director replied.

"This is the Heart to Heart Association, and we're calling to inform you that we now have a heart for Aleah Prim."

"That's great! Well not great, but you know what I mean," Doc corrected himself.

"We will be delivering it within the hour."

"Who was it, Doc? Who was it?" Shay asked.

"Well, Shay, brace yourself, we have found Aleah a heart," the director replied.

Shay was elated beyond belief. A man of many thoughts and many words, he was now speechless. He was ready to go.

"After the operation, you can see her," the director informed him.

"I cannot wait."

The surgeons awaited the heart. Pre-operative surgical procedures lasted approximately three hours and Shay couldn't wait to see Aleah. Shay walked into the room at 11:19 p.m.

The surgeons left the room to make the most unlikely call to the director.

"Aleah?"

"Shay?"

Aleah was stronger than any adult he's ever seen. He looked at her, more enamored than in prior days. He was wonderfully overwhelmed. Shay tried to hold back his tears, but he cried tears of great joy and reduced sorrow.

"Why are you crying, Shay?"

"You wouldn't understand, Aleah! You wouldn't understand!"

"Tell me!" Aleah muttered through her weak body.

"Just know that I love you so much, and I am just like super happy to see you and hear you and have a chance to continue making memories with you."

"Thank you…" Aleah paused. "Where's Mommy?"

"Hold up, beautiful, let me call her…"

Shay picked up his phone and discovered his missed call from Elizabeth.

He dialed her number and waited for an answer. He tried several times, but for some reason, she wasn't answering. "Hmm…I really need to reach her. She'd be so happy to know of Aleah's miraculous recovery."

He picked up his phone and tried once more. *Ring, ring…*

Once again, he received her voice mail.

29

—〰—

"Where's Mommy?" Aleah asked.

"I am not sure, but I will find out for you," Shay replied.

Shay looked at Aleah and smiled. There was no greater joy than a second chance at life. "I love you, Aleah! I love you too, Journey," Shay said as he began walking toward the door.

"Shay!" Aleah called.

"Yes?" Shay turned slightly.

"I love you too, Uncle Shay!" Journey interrupted. "I am glad Uncle Shay finally woke up!" Journey said to herself.

"I love you too," Aleah replied.

The moment was almost perfect.

Shay exited the room and turned left. He walked past Aleah's room and just so happened to take a look inside of the room next to hers. "Oh my gosh! This cannot be…" he paused as he looked at the person in the hospital bed. So many wires and on life support. Shay thought about his life over the past few days, and the stress of all he'd experienced was just too much. "I hope you die…" Shay said then put his hand on the plug. "You are selfish and evil. There is no good thing in you. You lack love and compassion. People like you should meet their maker as soon as possible to make the world a better place."

Shay held on to the plug and began disconnecting it from the wall when, much to his surprise, he heard, "Shay?"

Startled, he turned around. "Aleah, what are you doing out of bed?" Shay asked.

"What are you doing in this room?" Aleah stood at the door talking so she did not see who was lying there.

Shay quickly pushed the plug back in. "Nothing, I was just about to right a wrong, deliver a day of reckoning, you know?" Shay said to the man who had almost taken Aleah's life.

"No, Shay, I do not know, but let's go," Aleah said.

"Okay, Aleah, you need your rest, so I will be putting you back in bed then going to look for your mother," Shay replied.

"Okay!" Aleah said.

Aleah did not want to go back to bed, but she trusted Shay. Journey awaited Aleah's return to the room so they could finally talk again.

Shay helped Aleah to bed then continued walking around the hospital. He eventually walked back to Aleah's room for a quick check. She was doing all right. "Where the heck is Elizabeth?"

Aleah looked at Shay with a smile. "Have you found Mommy yet?"

"Not yet, but do not worry, I will."

Shay continued walking. His anger hadn't quite subsided regarding the kidnapper. He looked around then walked slowly toward the man. He now stood close enough to pull the plug. Shay put his hand on the plug once more, but before he could exact revenge, it happened, the man flatlined. He died right there in front of Shay's eyes, and there was a feeling of vindication then inexplicable sadness settled on him.

He hurried out of the room. He wiped a tear or two from his eyes then turned to walk left. Just up the hall, he saw a familiar face. He rushed over to her, "Oh my, Mrs. Prim, what are you doing he—"

Mrs. Elaine Prim turned and Shay beheld the hurt on her face "Hey, you do not have to cry anymore. Aleah is all better now and she is doing so well. Hey, do you want to see her?" He gave no conversational space to allow her to speak. Shay pulled Mrs. Prim's hand. She quickly stopped him though.

"Of course I want to see her. I was just about to go see her. There is something I must show you," Mrs. Prim said.

"Sure, what is it?" Shay asked.

Elaine stopped in front of the room. "Look at the person lying there," she said.

"Why are we doing this? We do not have time for a life lesson. I want you to see Aleah, and I am really trying to find Elizabeth," Shay replied.

Mrs. Prim lowered her head. "Go in and take a look," Mrs. Prim said.

"I am going to see Aleah now."

Shay began reluctantly walking as Elizabeth' mother began walking the other way. Shay looked at Mr. Prim then another great fear was upon him. He looked down at the girl lying in bed and grabbed her hand. "Elizabeth…no!" Teary-eyed once again, Shay stood at a loss for words. He stroked her hair as he frantically looked at Elizabeth then at the life support machine, back at Elizabeth then all of the wires. He repeated this process several times.

Life is but a vapor, here today and gone today. For many, tomorrow will never come and often we live for the next day having no knowledge of the fact that the present day will be our last. Unluckily for us, from the moment we are born, we begin our journey toward death. The greatest paradox of life is that we live to die.

The next sound heard summarized the most obvious definition of death—losing life! The high-pitched sound sent the room into panic. The tears solidified the anguish of the moment. They'd lost her, not just one of them—all of them. The nurses rushed in and other medical personnel moved quickly toward Elizabeth Prim. She laid elegantly with astounding beauty that no longer served relevant purpose.

They tried the defibrillators. The body jolted but remained unresponsive. Medical personal tried twice more, there was a glimmer of hope, but she flatlined again. They applied oxygen—unsuccessfully nonetheless.

Medical personnel shook their heads in sadness and began taking their masks and gloves off. "Sorry, we've lost her! I may need someone to call the director," the doctor said. They turned away.

"Hey, what is this child doing in here?" the nurse said in a stern voice. All of the three adults with whom Aleah was familiar began moving toward her.

"It's all right, it's Elizabeth's daughter." The recently-hired nurse began to cry.

"This is my granddaughter. It's okay," Mrs. Elaine Prim said.

Aleah looked at the bed in disbelief. She moved close enough to grab her mother's hand. The moment was solemn. Aleah, not yet fully aware of what was going on, began talking to her mother. "Mommy! Mommy! Wake up, Mommy, so that we can talk and play…" Aleah paused, but much to her dismay, received no response.

"I am fine, Mommy. I was asleep for a while, and I was hurting, but I do not have any more pain…" Aleah said joyfully then paused once more. "Mommy! Mommy!" Aleah began to worry and sadness joined her moment of joy.

"I love you, Mommy! I love you. I need you to wake up, Mommy!" Aleah held Mommy's hand tight and laid her head on her Mommy's body. She cried the deepest tears of desperation ever heard.

Everyone in the room looked on in disbelief and sadness.

Elizabeth journeyed toward Heaven's gates. God approached the pearly gates. "Welcome my child, my good and faithful servant!" God and the heavenly hosts smiled but then Heaven wept.

Around the time Elizabeth reached the white-and-gold gates, Aleah proclaimed once more, "I love you, Mommy!" Aleah said.

Elizabeth looked mildly surprised, smiled, and took in the scene in front of her. She looked at her sweet baby girl lying on her with one need only, love. She resituated a bit, "I love you too, Aleah."

Aleah looked. Elizabeth dropped a tear of joy. She looked at Aleah then toward Heaven. "Good-bye."

Elizabeth looked at Aleah once more then smiled. "My hero!" She closed her eyes as the room erupted in disbelief and wonder.

She flatlined for the final time, and the surgeons began making cuts around her heart.

Meanwhile, the phone rang. "Hello, Mr. Director!" the administrative assistant, Kelly said.

"Hello!" the director replied.

"We no longer need a heart for Aleah," Kelly informed the director.

"Why is that?" the director asked.

"Because she started breathing on her own. It was a miracle, Doc, a miracle!" Kelly said joyfully.

They disconnected the call. News traveled quickly, and the surgeons who operated on Elizabeth in order to save her own daughter, Aleah, ceased their operation.

"This heart no longer has a destination. We have to wait until we have a home for this heart before removing it," the head surgeon said.

Aleah looked at her mother. She was gone. They would never talk again, never play again, and they would never hug again. Shay and Elizabeth's parents cried.

Shay remembered the power of prayer and the power of love. "I love you, Elizabeth!" Shay said as he walked out of the room and began to pray.

"Mommy! Get up, Mommy!" Aleah cried.

"Pull that child away, Elaine!" Roger, her husband and father of Elizabeth, said sternly.

"No, Roger, I will not!" Mrs. Prim replied.

"Fine, then I will!"

Roger pulled, but Aleah held tightly to her mother. Eventually, Roger gave up. Aleah hugged her mother tight. She loved her mother and she would hold on to her until Heaven and earth collided.

Life is but a vapor, here today and gone today. For many tomorrow will never come, and often we live for the next day having no knowledge of the fact that the present day will be their last. Unluckily for us from the moment we are born we begin our journey toward death. The greatest paradox of life is death.

The next sound heard concluded the tale of the power of love! The high-pitched sound sent the room into a state of awe and wonder. The tears and smiles solidified the joy of the moment. God provided a second chance to her. They had gained an angel. The nurses rushed in and other medical personnel moved quickly toward the revitalized body of the young Elizabeth Prim. She laid elegantly with astounding beauty and a smile that demonstrated that of a grateful heart.

"Mooommmy!" Aleah yelled, smiled, and cried.

"My sweetest baby girl!" Elizabeth responded.

They hugged and kissed as the room stood amazed.

The director smiled. "Ah the power of love and the influence of faith! Our work is done here today. Two lives saved. Today was a good day!"

CPSIA information can be obtained
at www.ICGtesting.com
Printed in the USA
LVOW12s0004160916

504815LV00013B/58/P